TABLE 36

Linda Heavner Gerald

Cover by SelfPubBookCovers.com
Published by Lime Pie Publishing
Port St. Joe, Florida 32457.

ISBN: 978-1701058460

Published in the United States of America

The incredible spirit of the residents of Gulf and Bay Counties, you have been an inspiration. May God help you as you rebuild a new life. Each day appears easier with his help. To those who lost everything, keep the faith as you remain, #Port Joe Strong *on Twitter and* Port St. Joe Strong *on Facebook.*

ACKNOWLEDGMENTS

Surely as cream rises to the top, rose the love of this special town, Port St. Joe, as I worked on this book. So many wanted to help. Thank you to everyone who shared his or her personal story. I desired to allow some time for healing before releasing this book. Even without my planning it, the release day is almost the exact day our lives changed. Hopefully, *Table 36* will help bring a little closure. If I forget to mention you, please forgive me.

Dawn Lounsbury, many thanks for taking notes. I couldn't have gotten the timing right without those records.

Tim Croft, thank you for answering my pesky questions and offering assistance.

The following people contacted me with their stories. As it was too complicated to talk over the phone, these folks shared with me written personal accounts and information: Bette Wright Ashmore, Mary Ann Conroy, Mindy Pate, Riley Attila, Pauline Lantz, Gary Williams, Dena Gravatt, Angela Bivens-Anttila, Alyson Anttila, VieVie Baird, Mariann Ann Kelley Brown, Andi Ashmore, Colleen Burlingame, Deanna Gelak, Patricia Hardman, Susan McMillan Garrity, Barbara Rick Bertaccini, Natalie Dolan, and many others. Thank you. There were many more stories, but some couldn't send their contribution yet. For many, the pain is too much.

Table 36 is a combination of fact and fiction. I used the real names of places but changed the names of people. It makes the story more real if actual locations are written into the fiction.

PROLOGUE

Port St. Joseph, or Port St. Joe, began to prosper immediately upon its inception in 1835. That's when wealthy businessmen from Apalachicola decided to divert the cotton trade its way from that city, containing a shallow bay, which was not conducive for their business. The large ships necessary to haul their supplies of cotton needed deeper waters. These gentlemen decided that the harbor at Port St. Joe was kinder to the enormous vessels and that moving to deeper waters should expedite their trade. At that time, about twelve thousand people called Port St. Joe their permanent home, and this city was the largest one in Florida. Surrounding areas gazed lustily at the good fortune that came so easily to the Gulf County residents. *Why should our city leaders channel profits from us and make Gulf County more productive than Franklin?*

Governor Richard Keith Call assembled a group of delegates in Port St. Joe, Florida, in October 1838. The Constitutional Convention finally took place on December 3, 1838, with Robert R. Reid presiding as president and Joshua Knowles as secretary. The little town of Port St. Joe stood proudly, with a promising future, ready to prosper.

Three years later, only five hundred people, from the earlier twelve thousand remained to live and work in the beautiful area by the deep bay. In the year 1841, a deadly epidemic of yellow fever devastated the once-proud town. The final nail in the coffin, so to speak, occurred on September 8, 1844, when a massive storm arrived early one morning from the central gulf. It blew past Cape San Blas and made for the town of St. Joseph. The winds blew from the east, and hitting with great intensity, this monster continued inland as the winds swerved to the west. There were reports that the water in the bay was sucked out and added to the building waves that pummeled the shore. Recorded stories, from locals at the time, refer to this hellish occurrence as a "tidal wave," but it was not a tsunami. They are different phenomena.

After two days of struggling against this unforeseen cataclysm, the small coastal town barely remained standing. Houses were ripped apart as large trees were uprooted. Fortunes were lost as were numerous lives. Throughout Florida, the sad tale of the sudden end of a great city quickly spread. People traveled from all over the country to witness the horror and understand the massive destruction. Many residents, from local Apalachicola, rushed into the disaster area disassembling the few standing homes and moving them from St. Joseph to the town located only about twenty-nine miles away. Perhaps, fortune had beamed earlier on the Gulf County town of St. Joseph, but the residents of Franklin County now smiled as they reclaimed a position superior to their neighbors once again.

The Gulf of Mexico is not a stranger to massive storms. The Gulf and Bay Counties have been struck by several tropical storms and minor hurricanes over the years, but the two counties aren't even listed among the top ten regions of significant landfalls for hurricanes in the state of Florida. Only an average of one to two of these storms make landfall on the eastern coast of America every year. Unfortunately, 40 percent of these demons *do* hit other parts of Florida.

Port St. Joe, Florida, has borne more than its share of pain. Move forward from 1844, 174 years, to October 10, 2018. A similar event, once again, wrecked the beautiful beaches and destroyed most of the communities. The two storms appeared very similar. As it happened long ago, the winds pushed back the waters of the bay, sending them in massive swells onto the friendly sandy white beaches, which

TABLE 36

trembled at the impact. Gulf County stood shuddering, as it faced a formidable foe of winds recorded at 160 mph estimated intensity at landfall at Mexico Beach and Tyndall Air Force Base. This information was released later by scientists at NOAA's (National Oceanic and Atmospheric Administration) National Hurricane Center. However, you want to mark this giant, Hurricane Michael destroyed lives and fortunes just as the great storm of 1844. The significance of the winds is unquestionable, as, in 2018, residents stood again, not defiantly, but humbly asking God's help in reestablishing their way of life. Although many were forced to move, most of the inhabitants remained in hopes of a better experience moving forward.

Michael remains the first Category 5 hurricane to make landfall in the continental United States since Hurricane Andrew in 1992. The beach towns in Michael's path resembled a war zone as it raped the land. Almost a year after, residents shook their heads at how far they had improved in rebuilding lives. Secretly, tears of loss fell with memories at the way it once was in this beloved "slice of heaven." Since both Gulf and Bay Counties received mandatory evacuation orders as the storm approached, locals remained thankful that most of them obeyed these commands because what began as a Level One storm quickly intensified into sustained terrifying winds of a maximum of 161 mph. No one suspected such a sudden increase in wind and water.

Come any October, most residents in the hurricane paths of Florida relax a little from fears of a hurricane. Although October storms seldom occur, they can be cruel reminders that Mother Nature doesn't always follow the schedules of residents. Nine major hurricanes—those defined as being Category 3 or higher carrying sustained maximum wind speeds of 111 mph or more—have made landfall in Florida during the month of October since 1873. When Florida does get a significant October hurricane, most of them hit the southern section—or at least have in the last century. This one—Michael—tracked differently. Ninety percent of major storms to hit the United States between 1900 and 2000 occurred before October because the hurricane tracks move farther south in October, which creates a higher risk from the tropical activity for South Florida than any other part. Six Category 3 storms or higher have hit all Florida, while South Florida received the brunt of five of those strikes.

Michael rates as the third most intense Atlantic hurricane making landfall in terms of pressure; it only falls behind the 1935 Labor Day hurricane and Hurricane Camille of 1969. This latest monster, Michael, ranks as the first Category 5 hurricane on record to impact the Florida Panhandle, and the fourth-strongest in terms of wind speed. This information, obtained from several sources, demonstrates the intensity of winds facing residents in the impacted areas. When this monster ripped apart lives beginning at 2:00 p.m. on Wednesday, October 10, few could believe how drastically the little towns of Port St. Joe and Mexico Beach would change.

Such an enormous storm ranks as the thirteenth named storm and seventh hurricane of the 2018 Atlantic hurricane season. It began from a broad low-pressure area developing in the southwestern Caribbean Sea on October 1 and developed into a tropical depression on October 7, after being unable to intensify for nearly a week. Michael intensified into a hurricane near the western tip of Cuba, by the next day, as it moved northward. When the cyclone reached the Gulf of Mexico, it quickly grew stronger and was referred to as a "significant storm" on October 9. Even at that time, no one realized how strong it would become. An evolving beast, it finally reached Category 5 status as it swept into the Florida Panhandle with peak winds of 160 mph just before making landfall near Mexico Beach, Florida, on October 10. This fact made it the first storm, in this region, to be labeled as a Category 5 hurricane and the strongest storm of the 2018 season. Once Michael moved inland, it weakened as it took a northeastward trajectory toward the Chesapeake Bay. Over Georgia, the winds transitioned into an extratropical cyclone while it continued to move over southern Virginia late on October 10. The

TABLE 36

vast creature subsequently strengthened into a powerful extratropical hurricane and eventually impacted the Iberian Peninsula, before dissipating on October 16.

At least seventy-four deaths occurred in the United States and Central America due to this behemoth. Fifty-nine of these happened in the United States and fifteen in Central America, according to Wikipedia. Hurricane Michael caused an estimated $25.1 billion in economic losses including $100 million in Central America, with $6 billion at Tyndall Air Force Base alone. The area experienced at least $6.23 billion in insurance claims inside the United States, while losses in agriculture exceeded $3.87 billion.

The cities of Mexico Beach and Panama City suffered the worst of Michael along the Florida Panhandle due to the extreme winds and storm surge. Shocked residents stumbled back to flattened homes with trees felled over much of their land. Tyndall Air Force Base measured a maximum wind gust of 139 mph (224 km/h) that is before the sensors failed. Extensive power outages raged across the region as Michael ripped apart everything in the path it carved for itself. Life changed for everyone who lived in this gorgeous area.

The brave residents rapidly created social media bands of support on Facebook and Twitter to provide comfort and to remain connected. Just a small message of encouragement kept many focused as well as delivered sustainment. Everyone needed reassurance and help as they returned to awaiting nightmares. With all the repairs and rebuilding to do, workers came at a premium as hurricane survivors reported on good and bad experiences. All this proved to be a godsend to struggling homeowners.

As southerners, one thing we relish is our dining experiences. After damages were confirmed and loved ones reconnected, we longed for normalcy. When things at home go astray, aromatic smells and gentle laughter serve as beacons of comfort. After boisterous storms assail our lives, the returning luxury of strolling confidently inside to glasses tinkling with quiet toasts or hysterical laughter provides support.

Stress levels lower while we treasure our time with friends and community, which only these gatherings can offer. Without them, all of us would feel the blows of life more easily and more profoundly. Our favorite waitress's smile brightens our day and tells us that everything is in order. Once we return to "our restaurant," these joys of living soothe any anxious spirits despite the losses waiting back home.

This story of two small towns, named Port St. Joe and Mexico Beach, located in the Gulf and Bay Counties, Florida, is related to one of the favorite dining establishments of that region. Other restaurants proudly returned after much hard work and dedication, but this one place, Sunset Coastal Grill, will remain only in our hearts. Long lunches with groups of lady friends or fantastic dinners watching the purple sunset over a martini with beloved husbands now remain only fond memories. Precious meetings with the DAR (Daughters of the American Revolution) can never be held there again. All those days were ripped from our grasp by a monster named Michael.

Sunset Coastal Grill, we will, indeed, miss you and long for the days when you softened the load of our struggles. The brave and genuinely unique folks of Gulf and Bay Counties, Florida, may God continue to bless and keep you as we persist in celebrating life in one of the most beautiful locations on earth. Although we mourn the fate of those who perished, we refuse to cry for long. Instead, we desire to celebrate lives well lived and the indomitable spirits who still surround us. Maybe, the joy of living here each day requires sacrifices from those blessed enough to call this place *home*. Most of us feel our losses but continue to honor our God, who blesses us with another spectacular sunset every day. Table 36 will remain forever in the hearts of those who cherish those fading times before the annihilation of dreams, but we will search for another place on which to pin our future laughter because we have received a second chance.

1

In 2002, a unique table lovingly stood on the sunny porch of the newly built Sunset Coastal Grill located directly on the St. Joseph Bay in Port St. Joe, Florida. In this magical place, the sunsets each evening took away the breath of not only the tourists who loved this special place but the locals who rushed to enjoy lazy meals with family and friends. The building looked like a house. It *was* home to many as bright sunlight shafted into the porch windows at lunch or streaks of dazzling red and orange reflected from the waters that peeked through dark green palm fronds at another fantastic sunset. Inside, the pastel colors of the beadboard felt like the sea as tales of the "one that got away" caused joyous laughter from the group of small tables. Amid such mirth sat that special place, Table 36.

There wasn't anything outstanding in the appearance of the square four-seater table except that the sunsets appeared more vivid from it. Since it proudly stood in the center of the porch, diners seated there could see all the others. This little space stood by a tacky fake spindly evergreen tree decorated with cheesy ornaments and Christmas lights. That was the charm of Sunset Coastal. Nothing here received a great deal of planning. It just happened naturally, or so it seemed as customers left mementos of their love for the spirit of this place displayed on the tree.

Can you imagine all the stories this little table overheard as diners relaxed over another great meal or a bottle of wine? If only the walls could talk! If only those walls *still* harbored the small table. The raucous noise, from the Lion's Club, or the pledge of allegiance made by the sweet voices of the DAR, wafted through the air once each month in the larger room behind the porch. Many others scheduled weekly or monthly meetings as this soon became *the* place to meet. All the staff enjoyed the days when the Rotary Club or the Button Club held their meetings there. Laughter echoed inside the green-colored surroundings that housed Table 36. The local bridge club gaily chuckled over tales of family and friends as bids were placed with no thought that someday this place may not remain to house their memories. How could these gracious ladies know?

Just after the restaurant's opening, the glass doors, on the green building that blended so easily into the various trees and shrubs, welcomed a family of four. The tired group entered with large eyes and bewildered stares. This family of father, mother, son, and daughter had saved money and even asked help from family and friends to enjoy their first vacation. Seldom did they enjoy meals in a restaurant. The father was a simple factory worker while his wife stayed home with the children. Neither had a college degree but both worked proudly to provide every convenience, within their reach, to the children they loved.

This particular summer rated as the most difficult in the lives of this family. The parents had just received the disastrous word that their nine-year-old daughter, Cindy, would most likely not be present for another visit to the beach ever again. When the child first complained of pain in her joints, tiredness, and weakness, her parents didn't think much of such complaints. Were they even legitimate? Cindy wasn't an outstanding student like her brother, Jasper. Frequently, she staged illness to stay home with her computer. Her grumbling was swept under the rug with a soft chuckle from her dad.

One day, after Cindy returned from playing outside, her mother, Susan, noticed how deathly pale the little girl appeared. Susan grew

TABLE 36

concerned. She sat on the side of the child's bed and questioned her. The little girl was obviously not well. Susan softly hugged her only to find that Cindy felt unusually warm. Immediately, she phoned her husband, Peter, who instructed her to notify the pediatrician at once. Susan realized the need for restraint in spending money, even on health issues. This family's budget was usually tight and not nearly enough, so Mom always confirmed any medical calls first with her husband if that was possible.

Much too soon, after Cindy's checkup, Dr. Wilson phoned for the parents to come to his office. The Smiths knew it wouldn't be good news but couldn't prepare for the story that waited. "What is acute myelogenous leukemia?" Never had such a term been explained to the shocked parents who questioned the doctor, perplexed.

Dr. Wilson had experienced a stressful day, on that day of reckoning for the Smith family. Earlier, that same day, he'd lost one of his favorite patients and a dear personal friend. Dr. Wilson's threshold for sympathy had tanked. His lack of sympathy and compassion waited for these humble patients who failed to absorb his words. "It is acute leukemia. In simple terms, your child is dying. You waited too long to seek treatment. Many kids, with proper treatment, can live five years or longer." With complete lack of empathy, the young doctor turned on his right foot and strolled away with his head held high thinking only of the loss he'd just experienced while the parents felt guilty that they may have saved their daughter with quicker care. That was not the case.

Stunned, beyond feeling, the couple grabbed hands as they quietly prayed. In great confusion, they trouped away from this place of unkindness and death sentences. Later in the evening, they asked their sweet girl what she wanted to do most in the world. Knowing full well that they probably couldn't afford her request, they beamed when she replied, "I always wanted to go to a beach. Any beach would be so wonderful. Can we, Mommy? Can we really go?"

After many donations from family and friends, as well as constant saving, the family now enjoyed this incredible place of brightly colored purple sunsets, Tupelo honey, and white sandy beaches. Earlier in the day, their tired old gray Ford had limped into the little town of Port St. Joe. Immediately, they drove to Cape San Blas and watched with wonder as Jasper and Cindy, together, ran down the long white sandy beach. Grateful squeals filled the air as the two darted into the water or rolled gently in the sand. *So, this is the beach,* thought the young girl. It appeared more wonderful than she could ever have imagined! The laughter from their children should have brought joy to these parents, but they held each other tightly as tears ran down tired cheeks. How would they possibly deal with all this as they attempted to keep Cindy's spirits high? So much pain, it seemed impossible to bear.

The ending of such a special day deserved an excellent meal, so here they sat wide-eyed in the Sunset Coastal Grill at Table 36. They didn't know that this table was exceptional. "Please, watch your step," the older lady instructed the family as they stepped onto the porch and spotted the little table waiting for them.

"Oh, Mama, we have the best table," one of the kids proudly boasted.

Quietly, once seated, the Smiths shared unknown stories of the family's past because they were at last allowed time to relax with the kids. Laughter over something Uncle Ted did in his youth or Dad's maneuvers on the football field long ago provided a break from the stress. Such tales were never shared earlier with the children because, after all, there would be plenty of years ahead for relating these things. Dad usually felt too exhausted, and Mom plain beat, after long days with no help for all the chores at home. Suddenly, everything now looked hurried and vital. Memories must be quickly created since Cindy wouldn't be present with them for very long. No more putting things off or waiting to create precious family laughter. Each moment must be seized and enjoyed to the fullest.

Susan and Peter shared the spontaneous joy of their children, who laughed loudly at each other as they jeered over a hysterical memory shared by Dad. The small tap Jasper gave his younger sister's shoulder

TABLE 36

created another ugly bruise, but now there were many covering those spindly arms. Cindy attempted to pull her sleeve over the dark blue blotches on her pale arms covered with freckles. The youngster sported gorgeous red hair like her mom. Susan hastily wiped the tears from her dark green eyes etched in lines of worry.

"Mom, what's wrong? I know you, Mom. Since we've talked about coming to the beach, you seem so sad. Don't you like it here, Mom?" Peter and Jasper stared at the young mother who bowed her head.

"Yes, darling, of course, I love it here. What a perfect place, how could I not like the sun, sand, and water as well as experiencing all this with you? It is that I'm happy to be here with my family. I love you all so much." Her voice broke at this quiet explanation, which seemed to pacify the little girl as she traded jabs with her brother again.

"Jasper, don't hit your sister quite so hard. She bruises easily now."

"I know, what's wrong with Cindy, Dad?"

"Nothing, son, she just bruises easily. Like your mom." The tall sandy-haired man, with skinny shoulders, turned his blue eyes toward his wife as he overreacted to their innocent question. Susan was the rock of the family. Everyone looked to her for answers to hard questions and guidance each day.

Again, both kids turned to stare at the mother, who was saved by the approach of Bette, the waitress. This striking blonde's perky arrival and bright smile stopped any questions from the kids except regarding what they wanted for dinner. Dad's announcement surprised the kids when they were told to order "Anything you want." Usually, they received instructions that they must share a plate with warnings not to order anything expensive, but that didn't happen today. These parents decided that their children wouldn't share dishes or scrimp in any way, at least, not on *this* vacation.

"Really, Dad? What's going on?"

"Just living the good life, son. We are going to do that as long as we can." Peter's voice gagged with emotion as he glanced longingly at the blue-green waters of the bay. A large fish jumped for freedom from some menacing creature just as Peter longed for freedom from this horrible load and the uncertainty of his daughter's future. Eagerly, he stood before rushing away from the presence of those he loved. The experienced waitress watched this scene with great understanding. Her emerald eyes couldn't fathom what was happening, but she realized this family suffered from extraordinary events.

Frequently during their time there, Bette returned with funny stories and refills for drinks much more often than needed. After the meal, she returned with a small cake and a bright smile.

"Didn't I hear someone say something about a birthday? Well, you're in luck! Our baker just delivered several of these yummy chocolate cakes! Does anyone here love chocolate?" the waitress quizzed, as the reflection from the small pink candle burned bright in the eyes of the little child. How had this kind lady known to set the cake in front of the little girl and not the boy?

"*Is* it my birthday, Dad?" The child knew the answer, but the chocolate cake pulled her heart irresistibly. Her question was, "Is it okay for us to accept this cake even though it isn't my special day?"

The father gazed into the green eyes of Bette with so much gratitude. She nodded compassionately. A mom herself, she didn't mind paying extra for a little cake at the end of her shift. After all, what was life about if not to bring joy to precious children? Bette loved her job, bringing joy each day to her diners. Many asked specially for her.

"Yes, Cindy, it's your birthday. I hope each day will always be your special one." Her father's hand outstretched to the server was more than just a touch; it reached out with the hope that, just maybe, he could deliver what Cindy needed in her last hours. Table 36 experienced its first miracle of exceptional kindness in a room filled with fading golden light. There would be many more such acts of love and understanding in this place where dreams came true before the golden time was ripped away.

2

The next day, a local man, well into his nineties, slowly sauntered into the restaurant escorted by Vicky. Although the
Sunset Coastal Grill was a new place, he already had enjoyed
several meals there. Usually, Herbert ate alone. He had no family
members living close by. "Mr. Herbert, you know the drill. Watch
your step." The older man smiled sweetly at the hostess, who always
greeted him kindly.

The tall frail man lovingly braced the little table that had so easily
won his heart. Gently, he lowered himself into the chair, facing the
placid waters. Aging became more difficult each day. Herbert bowed
his head as he questioned where all his youth had disappeared. With
a quiet sigh, he shook his head. His favorite waitress, Sabrina, softly approached. His mind raced, considering a significant problem
threatening his life. Always, he faced up to questions, but this one
presented such a vital challenge to his very existence.

"Good afternoon, Mr. Herbert, I see you've come again. I'm glad."
Embarrassed, he nodded to the young woman barely out of her teens.
Such a youthful face, with large blue eyes, gazed at him. He recognized respect for the elderly in her humility. Mr. Herbert had a few
friends but seldom ventured outside at night. The quiet man spent
most of his waking hours, with his only remaining passion. Unknown
to most of the little town, the man of few words enjoyed a lucrative

position as an author of many famous books. He wrote anonymously for he hated attention. Few people took the time to learn about his skills or hobbies. To most, he was just another older man from a different place, who didn't appear very friendly. What they, unfortunately, didn't understand was that most authors didn't have time for lazy conversations or for playing games. When they bothered to venture into the public, their writers' minds were usually obsessed with correcting a sentence or completing the next chapter. Usually, people considered authors to be abstracted or downright weird, which was often true, but that was not always the case. There was a time when Mr. Herbert rated as the star quarterback at his high school located several states away. He had also worked, for most of his life, as the top salesman in a Fortune 500 company. He had won many awards and had accumulated great wealth from that period of his life.

After the death of his wife, Herbert had moved to this place of pink azaleas and yearly scallop festivals to enjoy the blue-green coastal waters and walks on long sandy beaches topped off with a perfect meal of fresh grouper when he desired. The sad part was that he had waited so long to venture to the coast. Wanda, his wife, of over sixty-seven years, had encouraged him to make that move long ago, while she lived, but the appeal of more money in his bank account and the prestige from company awards had been his only desire. Now, he felt old and alone without the support of his companion, who would have adored this place.

His only daughter, Jasmine, married a man who didn't care for him. The older man had attempted many times to win the respect of his son-in-law, but it had never happened. There were no visits from his only child far away. No grandchildren phoned with funny stories or requests for new Nikes. Mr. Herbert's only consolation was the books that he repeatedly dedicated to those he loved. Those books represented his children in his tired mind.

The old gentleman smiled brightly at the spunky girl who sat a large glass of sweetened iced tea before him. "Oh, wait, I forgot the lemon slices." Sabrina rushed back with the forgotten item. "Do you want your usual, Mr. Herbert? I don't mean to rush you. It's just that you always appear so hurried."

Mesmerized by the gentle satin waters and soft stirring of the great old palm tree, in the path of his gaze, he merely nodded. A sad and impossible obstacle faced the man who had accomplished greatness in everything that he did. If he had been a braggart, the entire town would have jockeyed for his attention, but that wasn't his style. Quietness and the same robotic routine completed the obsessive-compulsive tendencies he'd developed. Such was the way with most authors. It seemed these attributes enabled a writer to be more productive.

Several people arrived with smiles as they passed the private man with few words. The young waitress returned much too quickly with his order of Cajun shrimp. Herbert had hoped to have more time to think. The waitress thought her speed must please him, but not today. Searching for clarity, he decided not to leave this happy place until he had determined his fate. He smiled as the scent of the ocean from the oversized shrimp filled his nostrils. Slowly, he savored each flavor, not wanting this moment to end. Salty flavors, from a jumbo prawn, created a smile as did the thickness of a gigantic sea scallop. A decision must be made today if possible. Where would he end his life? His last days didn't show much promise as a future of blindness apparently waited for him.

Over thirty years ago, a much younger Herbert had received the diagnosis of macular degeneration. This progressive eye disease waited for most people as they aged, but genetics often hastened its arrival. Such was the case with Mr. Herbert. When the doctor explained to him long ago that he had most likely inherited this retinal problem, the possibility of enjoying a long life with few issues had still existed. Any symptoms his eye problem may create loomed far away in the future. *There's no cause for concern,* he had pondered back then. That long life had now run out for him. The day before, the good doctor said—that his sight was not likely to last long. Of course, he had prepared himself long ago for the inevitable. Always, he'd known the devastating news awaited him someday. Still, now that it was here, he found it difficult to believe so many years had flown past. *Where have they all gone? What will I do as a blind man?* Already, his central vision appeared blurred and hazy.

It is a good thing that I accumulated such a hefty balance in the bank. These facts made him smile. Maybe, he made the correct choice all those years when he'd planned and focused on achieving his goals. His many assets now presented him with two options: move to a high-end assisted-living facility or hire someone to live in his home and help him there. He hoped that he might find a reliable person, who didn't talk constantly so that he could continue living in his beautiful house by the water. The endless chatter of household help might interrupt his work or make it impossible to pursue his love. It would still be possible to pursue his passion for writing books with the aid of his computer.

Over and over, he challenged himself at solving this perplexing problem. This place, Port St. Joe, Florida, delighted his soul. Once he had settled here, the inspiration for his books had energized him as no other site had ever accomplished. The gentle surf daily outside his window on Cape San Blas and the salty air, which welcomed his senses each morning, were irreplaceable. How could he not receive inspiration from large swaths of purple and red each evening? It was difficult to go to bed as he wrote on his back porch to the sound of the night insects.

He smiled, remembering dinner invitations he had once received from prospective friends or invites to gatherings at the local pub with folks who wanted to share his life. Always, he'd chosen his quiet hours of being alone and writing. *It was my choice to remain alone.* He considered this as he wandered through his beloved coastal abode each evening. Now, he must face ending his days isolated.

As he waited for his slice of key lime pie, a pretty middle-aged lady, he'd often noticed around town, hesitantly approached him. "I don't mean to bother you, Mr. Herbert. Do you remember me? Mercia Hamel? Remember the day I saw you in the local bookstore? We spoke for such a long time. I was looking at one of your books. I can't recall which one." She smiled expectantly.

TABLE 36

Mr. Herbert nodded but had no *recollection* of such an event. "Anyway, you mentioned that you might need a housekeeper in the future. Well, that was over a year ago. Do you?"

The reclusive man felt irritated by this stranger's intrusion into his time, but he always felt exasperated by nonsensical chatter, his mind filled with more important things than daily jabber. "Do I what? I'm sorry." The older man realized his distraction must appear rude to the small woman who stood eagerly before him.

Mercia continued standing before Table 36 wishing that she could, maybe, fall through the floor. Other diners began to stare at this strange interaction. *Why doesn't he ask me to sit?* Again, she softly repeated her earlier statement, embarrassed at the stares of strangers.

Once, she had enjoyed life with her family. They had lived in a large house several miles away. Her husband's sudden death and the college expenses of her two children had depleted their bank account. Now, she worried herself to sleep each evening. *If only Mike were here, he would know what to do. My husband would never want me to go to work this late in my life.* She quickly wiped a small tear from her right eye. *Why is it the right one that always waters?*

"I'm so sorry, would you like to sit down?"

At last, he noticed me. Hastily, Mercia dropped into the chair facing the handsome older gentleman. Seated now, with her back to the crowd, she felt thankful for the chance not to be observed so plainly while she begged for employment. For the third time, she gently spoke the same words expressed earlier. Her tone changed as she explained that since the death of her husband of forty years, she found it impossible to pay the monthly bills. Her future hung in the balance. Already, she had moved into a small unattractive apartment. Desperation forced her to humiliate herself by approaching this stranger. The truth was that this man had never talked with her, except once. That had not been in a local bookstore but merely a nod in the grocery store. Never had he mentioned needing a housekeeper.

"Wait! What is your name?" A big smile from the quiet man caused Mercia to relax. Herbert flagged the server and ordered another large tea for his new friend, who briskly removed a wrinkled resume from her oversized brown purse. Her hands trembled as she passed it to him. The pink chipped fingernails didn't go with the immaculateness she otherwise presented. *This woman must be a hard worker.*

How many rejections have I received in my quest for employment? Desperation consumed her now. It was challenging to recall the number of times hope beckoned only to be passed over for a younger person. Mr. Herbert unfolded the tired piece of paper hopefully. The lady seated before him appeared humble and quiet. He realized, from her jewelry, that she had once not needed to beg for work. This dark-haired lady may be able to help him as much as he could help her. *Can it be that before me sits the answer to my prayer?* Of course, such an important decision required several interviews.

"Would you consider moving into a small apartment on my property? It is a carriage house, which I never even used. From it, you can witness the most striking sunsets in this world. I already employ a cleaner, so I will only need light cooking. At this point in my life, I don't eat very much. Are you a good driver? I need a driver for my book signings. Oh, we shall enjoy a great time if we can work out the details." As if he starved for information about her, his eyes quickly scanned the document.

Both of Mercia's eyes teared now. This time, she didn't bother to wipe her eyes because it appeared that both of Mr. Herbert's eyes also watered. "Sir, any place will be an improvement over the dingy place, I face each night. I never dreamed I might end my life in such a despicable place. To live in a lovely carriage house, watching these sunsets that you mention is my dream. Cooking is my passion. I do hope we can make it work."

Mr. Herbert nodded enthusiastically. "So do I."

The sweet young server, Sabrina, watched this promising interaction with great interest. *Why did all the neat customers always sit at Table 36?*

3

The buzz around the small town caused more people to reserve the little table. Table 36 was becoming trendy. Several days, after Mr. Herbert's lunch, an anxious young man arrived early for his 6:00 p.m. dinner reservation. He spied his reserved table, glad that his dinner companion hadn't arrived yet. Lovingly, he placed a single long-stemmed red rose in a lovely Baccarat crystal vase on the table and rushed to fill it with water. His dream was about to unfold. Everything had been neatly staged in his mind for months leading to this special event. Speeding back to his chair at the chosen table, he ordered a whiskey neat to calm his fluttering nerves.

An hour later, a young woman *finally* strutted proudly into the room, assisted once again by Vicky, who reminded her to watch her step as she entered the porch. As always, the sight of this dark-haired vixen took his breath away. Even though she was habitually an hour late for any event, Victoria was the most ravishing woman he'd ever seen. She was two inches taller than he was, which she often pointed out to him, but that didn't stop her from wearing the highest stilettos on the market. Tonight, the voluptuous lady was dressed in red with matching Louboutin's. Money didn't matter to the wealthy woman. But it did to Cabot Murphy, who was descended from a group of intellects that could not boast of wealth but only many degrees behind their names. He was aware that the family of the socialite didn't approve of him. The few times he received dinner invitations, he was reminded by her senator father that he didn't rate "up to par for *his* daughter." In fact, it had been a while since her family had acknowledged him. Still, Cabot adored the woman, who didn't bother to look at him, as she sat down with a grumpy sigh. Instead, she pushed back her chair, crossed her long legs, and critically appraised her surroundings.

"Let's just move this silly ole rose from the table. It looks cheap. I'm surprised that the restaurant would pick such tacky accessories for the table. Don't you, hon? Couldn't you have reserved a back table? That would have been quieter, you know? Isn't this place tiny? Oh my gosh, is that a fly?" Cabot motioned for the waitress so that he could ask for the back table just as another customer claimed it. The poor man always looked forward to spending time with the woman of his dreams but seldom did he enjoy himself. Maybe, he was in love with the version of the woman in his thoughts, not the actual one?

"I'm so sorry, Victoria. Perhaps, we can find a better table?" Scanning the room in a panic, Cabot realized the place was now filled. There were no empty tables. With regret, the handsome man looked into the baby blues of the dark-haired beauty with flawless ivory skin. He deeply breathed her French perfume, which he adored. Everything about her beauty pleased him.

"Well, next time do better, hon." He loved it when she called him *that* particular word reserved only for him. Never, had he heard her use it with anyone else. Victoria wasn't very affectionate, but he was hopeful that tonight may be different.

"Miss, please move the tacky old rose and this tacky little whatever tree. What is it with you people?" Victoria loved to give orders.

As the young waitress, Lisa, looked at the handsome man, she felt such pity for him. Instantly, she removed the rose and sat it on the bar. She motioned at the man, through the window, to where she had relocated it so that he might claim it as he left. Longingly, she smelled the heavenly scent of the old tea rose. No one had ever given her flowers.

TABLE 36

"Anyway, Daddy asked me to tell you that you embarrassed him terribly on the golf course last month. He said you *must* work on your game; it's lousy. Daddy probably won't be taking you to the club anymore after your performance. He also said that you need help with your wardrobe. Really, hon, you need to do better in so many areas. I'm sorry." Her bright red lips smiled at him as though she had uttered words of love. Cabot flinched. Victoria was known to be savagely brutal in her remarks, but he felt sure she didn't mean to be unkind. *Unfortunately, Daddy has spoiled his only child.* Sadly, he touched her face but quickly withdrew his hand.

"Tell me again why you picked this backwoods place to live? I don't get it. You really should move back to Dallas. Everyone there misses you. We speak of you often. I mean, what do you do here for fun, anyway?"

"Well, let's see, there's kayaking, boating, fishing, sailing, biking, tennis, beach walking, great restaurants, collecting unique shells, and the most beautiful sunsets from beaches with soft white sand, as well as all sorts of fun events plus genuine Tupelo honey made right here and tons of purple azaleas; what more could you want? Add to that the fact that many of the folks here are extremely talented. Just the music, supplied by the locals, will wow you. What's not to love?"

"Phew, all that requires walking through tons of gritty ole sand and getting all sweaty. That is unless you possess a large motor yacht? *Please,* tell me that you do. Maybe, you have saved it as a surprise? Daddy might change his opinion of you. Have you been hiding this from me, hon?" She smiled sweetly.

"Now, Victoria, you know that I haven't made my fortune yet, but I do have a job that will allow us to live anywhere in the world that we choose. We've discussed my salary many times. You know what I make and that I hope to receive a healthy pay rise very soon." He returned her smile.

Pouting, she puckered her red lips, which no longer appeared so lovely. Cabot gently took her hand. She quickly jerked it from his. "You know how I feel about public affection, hon. Every time we are together, I am forced to remind you of this. It's so weak and unbecoming. In fact, downright pathetic behavior if you ask me." She flashed him a bright smile from perfect teeth. He covered his mouth with his right hand. He was well aware that he couldn't return a spotless smile. His teeth still needed work. Daddy spent a ton of money on his only daughter giving her everything she desired except a "big ole yacht." Cabot smiled again.

The young waitress, standing back in the kitchen, begged anyone else to take these customers. It was apparent that the young woman, with jet-black hair, loathed her. Earlier, the customer had eyed her critically with a growl. None of the others were about to saddle themselves with *this* jewel sitting at the little space. *Usually, Table 36 harbors happy diners,* the small waitress thought.

With great trepidation, the woman, dressed in black shirt and slacks, approached the table with a huge smile. "You guys ready to order? Do you have any questions?"

"Yes, I have one. What's wrong with you? Why would you wear black slacks and shirt? You look ridiculous. Who dresses you? If you want, I can assist you for a nice fee. My design company helps struggling restaurants all the time. Didn't I ask you to move this silly ole tree? Anyway, you must use my designers. We'll fix you up, hon. Also, I have a great hairstylist. She could make you over, I think. You need a ton of work, hon. Do you even wear makeup? What's wrong with you?" Victoria's voice rose an octave, which meant she was becoming more and more frustrated with the actions of this server, but Victoria was accustomed to experiencing frustration with other women. Men were much easier for her to dominate. She took a deep breath as she tried to control her anger.

Cabot realized this was the first genuine smile he'd received from Victoria, whom he loved, and that she had used the particular endearment she used for him for the unknown waitress several times. *Isn't that her love term for only me? Is she trying to anger me?*

The girl in black rushed back to her friends sobbing. Lisa was deeply smitten with the handsome man with the stylish but rude

TABLE 36

woman. She observed them from the kitchen with tears in her eyes. They were what she thought of as "beautiful people." *Why was that wealthy lady so unkind? Did I do anything to provoke her?* Nothing came to her mind as she again begged the others to relieve her from this nightmare. The slighted girl even considered quitting right there. *Who needs this sort of treatment?* Then, she remembered her sick father at home and the mounting bills facing her and her mother. Taking a big breath, she again approached the "beautiful people" hoping for a kinder response.

"What you again? Can't we have a waitress who knows what she's doing? How many times must I ask you to remove this tacky thing? Please, get this ugly little tree out of my sight. Do you have a hearing problem or are you simply slow, hon?"

Hesitantly, the humiliated girl lifted the little tree and carried it to the back of the room. Other diners turned away sympathetically as she again wiped tears from her embarrassed face. Humiliated, once again, she marched back to Table 36, feeling scared and depressed. "Okay, mission accomplished! Ready to order now?"

"What is this a TV reality show? *Mission Accomplished?* How silly can you be? My friend here was telling me that I'm behaving in a mean way to you, but I don't respect silly old girls like you, hon, because I don't understand your lifestyle. Why don't you have a college education? Why demean yourself by serving others? Really, must you? Daddy and I may help you qualify for college if you even have such goals? Do you desire to be better than this?" Victoria used her right hand to motion in the air. Everyone looked at this loathsome person in disgust.

Although the young server believed in humility and kindness, her threshold for abuse had been crossed. "You know what? I *must* work because my father is dying. My seventy-year-old mother also works not because she loves her career, but because we may lose everything soon. Not everyone is born with a silver spoon in their perfect mouth. Do you want to order or sit here and embarrass your friend as well as everyone in this room? Why don't you let me know when you are ready? I'll be more than happy to take your order, finally!" The frustrated server sighed loudly as she marched away with her arms folded tightly over her chest. *I've taken enough abuse.*

"Cabot, did you hear the rudeness from this tart? I demand to see the owner at once. Your insolence will not be tolerated, hon. My friend is very powerful, and my Daddy is a senator. You are in serious trouble, Missy! By the way, you bring me a gin martini, shaken not stirred, with as many olives as possible on the side. I like six and make it snappy. I'm tired of dealing with you!" Victoria yelled her order.

Instantly, Lisa turned on her right foot. Angrily, she treaded again toward the kitchen, shocked that anyone could behave in such a mean way. This town did not accept rudeness from anyone. Seldom, did the locals experience such shocking behavior; only people from out of town would dare to behave in such an outrageous way.

"Victoria, honey, you're too hard on her. She's just a kid." Cabot's date looked hurt.

"Hon, you taking her side? I thought that you loved me." Again, she puckered her luscious full lips as she feigned sadness and batted her large blue eyes at him. Ordinarily, he would melt at that but not this evening. Her insolence had even begun to grate on Cabot like never before.

"You know, I love you more than all the money in the world and the gold in the sea." He often uttered the silly phrase to her because it seemed to make her happy. Tonight should prove to be too important to create a scene. He would discuss her rants at the restaurant tomorrow after tonight's request.

"Then, you are a fool! No one should love someone more than all the money in the world. In fact, I don't love you at all, Cabot. Did you never detect that? My plan was always to replace you when I found a better model, if you get my drift. I almost didn't come tonight because I feared you might create a scene when I tell you that I'm seeing someone else. Bart is tall and handsome, an ex-quarterback for Purdue. I'm sorry, hon, but you just don't cut the mustard. Plus, Daddy hates you, you know? When you moved to this silly ole town, I

TABLE 36

began to shop for a better model if you catch my drift." Victoria snickered as she repeated the expression she had used earlier.

"Yes, I do. I always hoped that you cared for me, but I always knew it was a pipe dream." Cabot lowered his head in desperation.

"What a silly phrase! *A pipe dream.* Where do you invent these dumb sayings? Maybe, you should get together with the little waitress. You two could hold hands and show public displays of affection. Wouldn't that be peachy? Well, I need to leave now. I'll be late for my flight. I have to drive all the way back to that tacky town, Panama Something. I do hope that you enjoy your simple life in this Podunk place. Tell the little waitress, what's her name, that I won't need the drink, hon. You look like you may need it more than me!" The wicked woman stood up.

Standing inside the door, the waitress watched all this. Lisa stepped down just as Victoria approached with great haste. The determined girl was carrying a tray of drinks; she missed the step, which propelled the martini through the air right onto the bright red Chanel jacket of the exiting lady. Victoria screamed loudly. "You idiot! I'll be calling the owner tomorrow! You are a complete loser! Do you have any idea about the price of my jacket? Are you going to pay for the cleaning bill? *No, because you can't afford it!*"

"There's no need for that. I am the owner! One of the other girls phoned earlier when you started this obnoxious scene. What sort of bully makes a young girl cry? I came back to my restaurant to ask you to leave. You are not welcome here. Just, please, leave!"

Victoria stomped away as the other diners stood to applaud. The dark-haired lady stopped at the step to glare at them all one more time before knocking everyone in her way aside.

"Bravo! Bravo!" The standing diners applauded the words of the owner.

Cabot motioned for the embarrassed girl. "Do you mind if I show you something? I was going to ask that bitch to marry me. Look at the ring that I have worked for many months to purchase. My dream was to surprise her. You have saved me from a life in hell. What was

I thinking? Although she is the most beautiful woman in the world to me, how could I not see her hatefulness until now? Can I ever find words to thank you? Your kindness only reinforced her rudeness," he said softly to the young lady, who nervously glanced around the room.

"You may not think of me as kind when I tell you that I orchestrated the entire fall. I hoped that the drink might land on her face, but it was pretty good where it landed on her fancy jacket. Your ring is lovely. Don't worry; you'll find someone else to share your life with."

Cabot gently squeezed her hand. "Yes, I'm sure that I will. Do *you* date anyone? Maybe, you will consider going out with me when it's convenient. I live here, in Port St. Joe now, so you'll be seeing a great deal of me if it's okay." Diners around the small table smiled with lowered heads as Cabot rapidly returned with the lovely red rose, which he handed to Lisa. *What was it about Table 36?*

4

"Grandmom, you sure you can climb a structure that is ninety-six feet and one hundred thirty-eight steps? I'm not calling you old, but that's a lot of stairs for anyone, especially for someone your age." The young lad looked at the older woman with awe. He loved her so much.

"Yes, you remember, William, I've told you. I did this last summer with Uncle Don. Will you stop worrying about me?" The older woman walked between a young man and a younger girl.

William, the handsome thirteen-year-old boy accompanying the two females, stood at almost six feet even at this young age. His shiny brown hair and satiny dark eyes made everyone turn twice to see him. His sister was a petite version of him, while Grandmom looked younger than her seventy-eight years.

William shook his head at their grandmother, who awed the entire family with her wit and energy. The waiter, Bill, escorted them onto the sunny porch. "Please, watch your step."

The older woman smiled as she rushed past the waiter to the waiting table, her favorite one, Table 36. Quickly, she lowered herself into the straight-backed chair facing the churning waters outside on this blustery, cloudy day. Usually, entertaining her two grandchildren was simple, but on days like this, it required ingenuity to keep them busy. The two children had just arrived from Minnesota. So many

21

fun adventures waited on sunny days, but days like this weren't so easy. Grandmother Little was grateful for the new location of the lighthouse, which would only provide another joyous afternoon's diversion.

"You know, since they moved that old lighthouse from Cape San Blas into the town, many people enjoy it. Do you know much about the history of it?" The question was posed by the waiter. Bill loved to talk with visitors to the area. He was a seasoned server with years of experience at various places.

"Oh yes, indeed we do. The children have studied it since their arrival yesterday. This cloudy, windy day seemed perfect for a visit there. These kids are ready to climb. Say, why don't you tell us what you know, Bill? Maybe, you can add to our knowledge. They are always eager to learn new facts. Right, kids?" Both nodded eagerly as they beamed at the young server.

Bill responded immediately. "Well, let me see. Do you know that it was completed in 1849 with a budget of eight thousand dollars? You do know that? Umm, well, did you know that a gale in 1841 ripped it apart? You also knew that? Okay, what about that the new structure was then completed in 1856 for twelve thousand dollars? You knew that too? Well, did you realize that a horrible storm, in August 1856, devastated the poor thing again?" The children yawned as Bill scratched his head. *This group is difficult to impress.*

"Obviously, you do. How about the damages perpetrated in 1862 during the Civil War that badly destroyed it again!" Bill's eyes gleamed as he faced his challengers. He felt sure this must be a new tidbit for the family, but the kids strolled over to the windows as though searching for the gleaming white old tower. They ignored him, shaming him in his effort to help.

"Children, how rude can you be? Mr. Bill is kind enough to share his facts. You be gracious and listen. Right now, William and Eileen!" They strolled back glaring at the handsome waiter.

"Mr. Bill, we know all that. Don't you know anything that we don't? We are both advanced students, so you may need to study your book."

TABLE 36

They giggled while giving high fives to each other over the head of their grandmother.

Mr. Bill was beginning to regret offering to share his facts but dug deeper into his memory. "You probably were aware that on July 3, 1832, Mother Nature uprooted that cone-shaped building. Finally, on July 30, 1885, the fourth tower, just a skeleton of iron, stood proudly. Two dwellings shrouded it for the keepers; they added security to the entire scene. Everyone thought it would never fall again! Two years later, only two hundred feet of beach remained. You guys can't know all this? The only reason I do is that my grandchildren just visited. I always brush up on local history before their arrival. Like you two, mine also love that mysterious white magnet of hope that sits so close to us now. What a history it harbors! Okay, let me add this, the powers that were, back then, decided to move our lighthouse to Black's Island in St. Joseph's Bay. Let's see; here my facts become blurred, but I do know that the tower moved again in 1919. Whew! That's it; I can't add much more than all that. Anyway, that delightful building has moved at least four times maybe more to mark the southern point of Florida's Cape San Blas. I'm exhausted. Maybe, you need to talk to the nice lady at the keeper's quarters museum. I'll bet she can challenge your knowledge. She knows everything there is to know about that lighthouse!" He sped away.

Soon enough, Bill returned with a tray carrying three sweet iced teas and lemons. He smiled, warmly at the little table. "I phoned my grandson, Austin, who reminded me of something you may not know. Are you aware that our lighthouse is haunted?" Now, he had their attention.

William knocked the large glass of iced tea over as soon as he reached for it, which spilled onto his sister's lap, who screamed loudly. Everyone in the peaceful room stared at the usually prim Table 36. "No way, Mr. Bill! You're making that up because you ran out of facts. We never read anything about any ghosts, and we've really studied up on the facts."

"Well, the locals know all about it. You should read some more on this detail. Then, visit it for a full moon climb. I'll bet you'll be scared to death. Pardon the pun. In fact, I'll challenge you to climb it at night once you know the truth!"

Mrs. Little, who had lived in Port St. Joe all her life, wondered why she hadn't thought of that fact. She had known about the rumor of ghosts roaming around the ancient lighthouse since her childhood. The elderly lady realized that her grandchildren would never forget a spooky climb up all the stairs of a haunted tower! She planned to check on the date of the next full moon for the climb. *It certainly won't be tonight*, she thought as she stared at the mounting whitecaps on the water.

"Do you remember any more details about these ghosts? Your memory is really great, Mr. Bill." The children now couldn't get enough of Mr. Bill and his ghostly facts.

Bill shifted his weight to his left foot while considering how he could recall all the scary rumors. At his age, he found it difficult to state facts in perfect chronological order. His grandson had reminded him about the lighthouse's haunted history but hadn't provided any circumstances. "Boy, you're a hardcore group, but, yes, I do recall a little. Mr. Marler died a terrible death there. They never found the perpetrator of *his* murder, but all sorts of rumors spread at the time in 1938. After his death, Mr. White reported hearing moaning and heavy breathing in that tower."

Both children huddled around their grandmother, who grabbed Bill's black shirt. "Another keeper committed suicide in 1932, probably due to loneliness or maybe the ghost of old Mr. Marler." Bill used his scariest voice to relay the latest news as he stared at the churning waters outside. He moved his hands in the air in a ghostly manner.

"Mr. Linton then entered the scene as a kind man, who saved a few lives during his stint at the old Cape San Blas Lighthouse. I would have liked to know him." Bill looked longingly at the churning waters rushing onto the shore.

Another diner approached angrily. "Hey, you do have other customers. What's wrong with you today, Bill? You usually don't waste time like this. You kids, stop dominating our waiter!" The befuddled

TABLE 36

waiter dashed behind the complaining man but quickly returned. Bill loved children, and these two were delightful.

"Where were we? Oh yes, Mr. Linton's sad demise. Next, two painters, who tied themselves with ropes as a safety measure, plunged one hundred feet to their death. You tell me how this could happen? Those men secured themselves with heavy lines. The unexplained deaths continued on October 8, 1957. At that time, two more men died unexplainably. They were two coast guards who strangely disappeared from their post at the lighthouse. Only a few of their belongings remained. Reports of two skeleton figures strolling down the beach really shook the residents. Late at night, I still search the roads for them. Every time I see a moving light, I think that, maybe, it's them carrying a lantern. As you can see, even one of these tales forms grounds for a reputation for sinister occurrences, but all this? There are probably other stories, but my memory, which you earlier praised, is not really so great."

The kids hung their heads. Bill completed his grim recantation by adding, "Perhaps, all these weird events are over, but if you ever brave the full moon climb, well, you'd best be careful." He turned and strolled away with his head down.

As the children, solemnly chewed their chicken strips, they stared at the angry waters outside. "You know, Grandmom, I don't think we want to do the full moon climb on this visit. Maybe, next year. We should probably wait a few years before tackling it."

Grandmother nodded in agreement while pondering this re- markable place of exciting people, complicated history, and a little table where children received tales to inspire their love of the past.

5

S he knew. What the waitress witnessed made her hair stand on end. The young server knew because she had experienced the horror, but with help from friends and a great deal of bravery, she had escaped.

"Darling, watch your step! Here, let me support your arm a little. Is it still painful? I don't want you to worry about anything." The man's kindness appeared overwhelming as he lovingly guided the young woman to an awaiting reservation at Table 36. Gently, he kissed her as though she may break. Other diners smiled at the love of this man for the lady who was apparently his wife. Even after months of meals served to the residents of Port St. Joe at the Sunset Grill, the little table was the most requested. What was it about the small space that made diners frequently ask for it?

"Isn't it a beautiful day, Deanna honey?" The man touched her arm gently, but the woman jumped dramatically at his touch. Quickly, she averted her eyes from his stare. The waitress approached with a grin as she barely looked at the "kind" man. She knew what a monster he was. Her eyes looked into the very soul of the sad woman named Deanna.

The tiny diner managed to return a smile as she breathed deeply. This delicate lady was petite. Her short brown hair, cut dramatically close, looked dull and drab. The brown eyes she raised were filled

TABLE 36

with sadness; there was no light shining from them. Dark circles and swelling gave the stranger's bruised face a surreal appearance. Just smiling created so much pain in her damaged right jaw. It appeared she was unable to look at the man who kept rubbing her shoulder with so much love.

What liars they both are! The waitress wanted to hit the bully, but she knew it would accomplish nothing except the loss of her position, and she desperately needed this work. Her husband, Jason, had lost his job four months earlier. There weren't many places of employment available in Gulf County. So, she smiled sweetly and watched the miserable couple's vain attempt at interaction.

"May I take your drink orders? Are you on vacation here?" The question appeared innocent enough.

Deanna appeared to perk up a little as she gazed into kind green eyes that seemed to try to speak to her. *Can she know? Of course not!*

The man, Carl, glared at the intruding waitress as if he wished she would disintegrate. Chatty women always presented a challenge to the man. If this stranger encouraged his frail wife to speak, what might the idiot share in her condition? The assault had just occurred. He was crazy to have taken the risk of exposing his weak wife to inquiring busybodies. The only reason he had was to shut his wife's mouth from her crying. Carl found it difficult being around her for very long.

"Yes, indeed, we'll both have unsweet tea without lemon. Thank you, but we're not ready to order yet. Why don't you run along? We'll let you know when we want your service. My wife and I just want to be alone. We are so in love, right, honey?" His words reverberated with a snarly sort of growl.

I'll just bet you don't want lemons. You are sour enough without them! the waitress, Anna, thought as she smiled at her own wit.

Purposefully, the understanding employee rushed back to the table without their summons after only a few moments. "Here, I am again!" Anna exaggerated her sweet smile to annoy the arrogant man. It worked.

"Didn't I ask you to wait until we summoned you? *We don't want to be rushed* if you don't mind."

Oh, he's clever. The challenger returned his fake smile. The domineering husband understood what was happening and didn't like it one bit. He even considered leaving but didn't think this could amount to much. How smart could this quirky waitress be?

"Did you? I didn't hear you. My attention was focused on the large bruise on your wife's small arm and under her eye. Ouch! That must be painful. What a horrible thing to happen on your vacation." She pointed dramatically at the arm. Other diners turned to observe.

"Yes, you're right about that one. My sweet wife fell down the stairs in our rental unit last night. It was awful. Deanna loves her whiskey sours, right, darling? She tends to overdrink. Oh well, no one's perfect, right? If only you knew about all her blunders." The woman blushed at his lie but turned her eyes away from him with a sad, gentle nod.

"You don't say. I once experienced such falls and bruises but made a life change, and they instantly stopped. Now, isn't that strange?" The waitress's lowered voice could only be heard by the two diners sitting at Table 36. Deanna became agitated and very anxious. Her husband hit the table with his fist, not loudly to call attention to them, but to demonstrate that he was in control and would not be harassed by what this person might *think* she knew.

"What's your name? Aw, yes, Anna. You listen carefully to me. I don't know what you *think* is happening here, but you best be careful. Our condo isn't far. I might show up here, later tonight, and you may not be so pesky then!" Anna got his drift but refused to back down.

"I'm sure you might, but my six-foot-four-inch husband always picks me up and loves a challenge. However, you wouldn't be anything but a fly to him. Of course, you wouldn't dare to confront him. Deanna, or I, am more your speed to bully. Are you ready to order, sweet lady?"

No one had ever confronted Carl before, at least, not in the wife's presence. She didn't know how to respond. Deanna knew the waitress

TABLE 36

meant well, but her time of abuse had cycled. Now, the monster, sitting to her right, would treat her kindly until he drank too much, or something she did, again, happened to set him off. Then, her husband would come for her with hate and anger. Each time she thought he changed, the disappointing reality jolted her into the realization that he never would.

They both ordered a burger, but Deanna considered that the pain in her jaw might prevent enjoyment. A few tears oozed out of her swollen purple eyes. Quickly, she wiped them away. *If Carl sees me cry, he will become outraged. He may even harm the kind waitress or other diners.* Thank goodness, the culture was changing. Spousal abuse was harder to commit; people watched out more for each other.

"You okay, honey? You aren't crying, are you?" His voice was rising, which wasn't a good sign; this usually meant that he was upset. "That bitch of a waitress better watch herself. Do *you* get my drift? She's beginning to annoy me. Now, you know what that may mean, don't you darling?" Deanna refused to look at him. He could easily make her leave. If they went home, while he was becoming angry, his wrath would build on the way home. What waited for her would not be pretty.

Oh, no, here she comes again. Why won't she leave us alone? Doesn't she know that she's only making things worse for me? How could she know? Anna knew quite well what was happening at Table 36 and what she was doing.

"I need to go to the ladies' room, Carl. Be right back." The wife suddenly felt emboldened by the nod of the waitress and the fire in her emerald eyes. Gently, Deanna touched the monster's right shoulder. It was imperative that she not arouse his suspicions. The controlling man hated for her to leave his side when in public. Her action could prove disastrous if the frail woman encountered time alone with that screwy waitress. He glanced around the room, making sure no other diners watched.

"Your burgers will be right out." The gutsy waitress turned to rush to the ladies' room behind Deanna. Now was her chance.

"Where are you going in such a hurry?" Carl grabbed her by the right arm and pulled her back to the table.

"I just received a signal from the kitchen. I'll be right back, honest." Quickly, Anna turned to a customer. The tall man was a local friend and also from law enforcement. Today was his day off. God surely was orchestrating this event.

"Cliff, long time no see! How's everything? Had any more trouble out of that couple next door?" Cliff was exemplary at his job and a good reader of people. He knew that Anna was sending him a message but was taken aback. Several seconds passed as he tried to understand.

"Let me introduce, Carl. His lovely wife, Deanna, will be back in a moment. It seems she fell down the stairs last night. Several bruises and bangs are visible. Isn't that sad? Sort of like those other tourists next to you, eh? These things seem especially worrisome when a woman is away from family and friends. I'll be right back with your order, Carl."

Cliff sidled up to the seated man. He didn't smile any longer. "Where you folks staying? You know, this place is a small town. I'll do a tag check on you as you leave. Your wife sounds like she's accustomed to falls and other injuries. In this town, and all over the south, we watch for women who are frequently injured. You never know when they might fall and need us. We try to be around. Do you understand?"

Anna rushed into the ladies' room. "Deanna, I know what's happening here. I was married to a bully who beat me up one too many times. The best thing I ever did was getting away from him. Believe me, I know how hard it is. You're afraid, of course, but I also know if you don't leave him, *now*, he may injure you or much worse. He may even kill you. It happens each day. I'm begging you, let me help!"

The confused and scared woman fell onto the tiled floor as she choked on her tears. Black mascara streaked down a china-doll face. Gingerly, she held her swollen jaw. "I just can't leave my husband. Where will I go? What will I do? Carl always tells me that no one will

TABLE 36

care about me except him. He's the only person who loves me. I don't have a family anymore. Believe me, I know my actions are weak but I'm so scared. I've dreamed of this day. Of a savior to help me. Now, that it's finally here, I find myself unable to leave him." Her gentle sobs became hysterical as she grabbed onto the dark slacks of the kind older woman.

"You now have me to help. I will deliver you from Carl's evil clutches if you'll only let me. Allow me to walk out of here with you. There is a law enforcement officer outside by your table. It's his day off. He always comes this time of day on Wednesday. Table 36 is his favorite station. When I left, he was talking with Carl. Cliff will help us. Deanna, let us assist you. You don't have to live like this anymore. Imagine, waking up free from Carl's insults and abuse. I'm begging you; please, let us help you. There are homes for abused wives and children in the area. If I did it; you can free yourself of this maniac." Excitedly, Anna pointed at the door. Minutes felt like hours as the two women stared into each other's eyes. Anna knelt to the floor beside the younger woman. Gently, she took her left hand. This time was crucial. There may never be a chance for Deanna to free herself from Carl's tentacles, but the abused wife needed strength, which she obviously didn't possess.

"Deanna, may I pray with you? This moment may be the only one you have." The hysterical woman's tears ceased as she nodded acceptance.

"Please, Lord Jesus, help Deanna. Give her the strength she needs. You tell us to be brave and courageous. She needs that from you. Please, Jesus." Again, the two women stared into each other's eyes. The small woman slowly stood. Boldly, she took the hand of Anna.

"Lead the way! Free me from the pain. I can't take it anymore. I think my jaw is broken. It hurts so badly. I am scared beyond belief." The waitress felt the smaller woman shaking. Her palms were wet. The two women approached holding hands as Cliff immediately walked away from his steak dinner. With gentle arms, he shielded Deanna. The little woman managed a bold smile.

"Officer, will you please help me? My name is Deanna Townsend; this man, Carl, is my husband. He is abusive and has been for several years. I can't take it anymore. My jaw may be broken; will you take me to a hospital? If this man ever approaches me or tries to contact me, I'm gonna turn you loose on him. For now, just get me away from him. I can't be any braver than that, not yet." Although she continued to shake, new confidence exuded from her face.

Deanna turned to face her abuser with such boldness that the waitress gasped. As the small woman looked into the eyes that had caused her so much pain, she didn't back down. Finally, Carl looked down in exasperation. Cliff escorted a brave survivor as she slowly walked away from years of madness.

Striding toward Table 36 and the whimpering man, Anna thanked God for hearing her prayer. "What more can I get you, *Carl?*"

"There's nothing more you can do."

"Then, please leave, right now." Carl slinked away.

6

Slowly, the years trickled past in Port St. Joe. Residents assumed their way of life would remain the same. How could they realize that a monster would soon form out in the gulf? Soon, their way of life would be no more.

During mid-August, 2017, the kids returned to school, but the hustle and bustle of many tourists remained due to the advent of the scallop season. The tiny bay scallops developed rapidly from eggs into larvae within thirty-six hours of fertilization. After that, these veligers settled at the bottom of the water. They remained there for the rest of their lives. The tiny blue eyes of the delicate mollusks, acting as detectors, helped guide them as they floated in the usually gentle waters of the bay. Often, they were scooped up by hungry diners who combed the clear spaces in search of these delicate morsels.

Interestingly, these creatures proved to be excellent indicators of the environment since they preferred to live in pristine waters. This unusual fact made them desirable to eat. During scallop season many strangers invaded the area in search of lunch or dinner that quietly floated inside the waters of the bay. They were very small so collecting enough for a meal proved a challenge.

"I told you that I want to eat at Joe Mama's! Why do we have to come here, Dad? You and Mom always get to do what you want."

"That's true, Mom. Remember, I told you, before we left home, that I wanted to eat at the Indian Pass Raw Bar. I love that place, but no. You force us to come here. This place is too fancy for me."

"You know what? Let's all just go back home. How does that suit everyone? Mom and I bring you to the place that you talk about so often, and all you do is complain. Can't you ever just be happy? Don't you think that we should be able to enjoy ourselves too? You are both selfish. Let's turn around, right now, and drive eight hours home. Maybe, then, you'll be quiet and stop complaining!"

Glenn Parker sighed loudly as he stood at the top of the little step. His wife, Mabel, and the two children, Howie and Hilda, groaned angrily. The family felt disgusted that after driving such a long way they hadn't yet found a single scallop. Everyone was extremely hot on this long August day and needed to relax. What began as an exciting three-day vacation to the coast had become a drag on everyone. Their waitress, Judith, also stood at the top of the small stair holding menus for them if they decided to stay.

"Did you ever think that we can go to your favorite restaurants tonight or tomorrow or even the next day? We're going to be here for three more days, but I have no intention of enduring this bickering. If this is the way it has to be, I want to go home! I feel tired and distressed as well as you!"

Mabel nodded in agreement with Glenn while Judith continued to wait patiently for their decision. She sighed gently. Everyone knew that the Parker family was not about to turn around and drive eight hours back to their home, but it made a good defense for obtaining peace from the arguing kids. Slowly, the minutes ticked away as the family waited. Other diners, sitting on the sunny porch, turned to stare as they also waited for this drama to play out. Everyone with kids recognized this scenario as the much-awaited family vacation turned sour due to tiredness and flaring tempers.

Finally, Howie pushed his sister, Hilda, onto the porch. "Oh, let's just have lunch here. I can wait till tonight to have dinner at *my*

TABLE 36

favorite place, Joe Mama's." He smiled at his sister, who staggered to regain her step.

"No way! I'm having dinner tonight at *my* favorite restaurant, the Indian Pass Raw Bar. I haven't been there in three months."

Glen and Mabel continued to stand on the top step as Howie joined his sister on the porch. Light flooded the space, as the bay outside shone, beckoning everyone to "just chill and enjoy life." What a perfect day, even though this was typical August weather boasting extreme heat and humidity. No wonder the little family was grumpy. Poor Judith, smiling, waited without a word for the parents to speak. She wasn't surprised at this family drama. When you worked as a hostess in a resort town, one came to expect such arguing even from the most-loved family members. No one moved.

"Fine, let Howie eat at Joe Mama's tonight. I'm used to never getting my way. I always have to be the one who bends to all *your* wishes." Hilda pushed her brother toward the little four-seater table, which they always reserved when dining at the Sunset Grill. Her parents smiled gratefully as the hostess gently reminded them, "Watch your step. Welcome home, Parker family. We have missed you."

Mr. and Mrs. Parker doubted Judith's kind words since their kids had disrupted everyone's peace on this sunny day marking the beginning of the scallop season for 2017. Usually, their children displayed good manners with happy smiles, but this heat and humidity would cause anyone to turn irritable.

Once the four eventually sat facing the tranquil waters, tempers soothed, and kindness regained its place. The experienced waitress rushed four large sweet iced teas with plenty of lemons just the way the Parkers always requested. Lovingly, she sat the heavy glasses in front of each. She smiled warmly at the little family, who finally appeared to relax. This manner was what they usually exhibited when dining on the porch.

"Oh, wow, did you see that gargantuan fish jump out of the water? What do you think is chasing him?" Howie's eyes beamed with excitement. Glen smiled fondly at this young man whom he loved with all his heart.

"Duh, probably Jaws!" Hilda ran over to the large sparkling window. Her eyes never veered from the scene outside. She was hooked on the story of *Jaws* and refused to get more than ankle-deep in the waters, which made scalloping something of a chore for the others. This family was filled with love and respect not only for each other but also for the environment. Carefully, they always ensured that the beach was clean and in better condition than they found it. When they walked the beach, each member carried a trash bag, which they tried to fill with debris. Although the beaches on Cape San Blas were pristine, tourists often didn't understand nor appreciate that it was their responsibility to care for this jewel that the Great Creator gave to everyone.

Quiet small talk died as soon as the food arrived. No longer did gentle jabs at each other and braggart attitudes dominate. The bold taste of fresh grouper caused their weariness to wane. The two kids transformed into responsible, easy-to-love young adults while their parents smiled at each other with big toothy grins. Judith stood on the small step watching this transformation from a quarreling family to a family of peace, with great pleasure. No wonder she loved her job and the people who not only lived in Port St. Joe but returned several times each year to thrill at its beauty. This scene was merely another day in paradise, she thought. Surely, it would last for a very long time.

7

How quickly the month of August 2017 sped past, bringing September the month everyone at the coast dreaded. This month was the prime time for hurricanes. Residents breathed a sigh of relief when October finally arrived. Yes, October was still considered hurricane season, but the gulf seldom received massive storms that late in the year. October always rated as one of the most treasured among the months. The temperature and humidity fell, making it delightful to enjoy the outdoors. This particular October of 2017 appeared glorious.

"We are delighted to see the four of you. So, how's the Blast on the Bay Songwriter's Festival going? Are you excited? Watch your step, but you already know all this." Ein, one of the servers, lightly touched the arm of one of the slender girls who was regarded by the community with great love and respect.

"It was going great for us, but we've hit a snag. You got any inspiration for us? We only need one more song to complete our list but, man, it's hard to be inspired after being holed up for three days in her studio." Softly, the dark-haired beauty referred to their predicament as she pointed to the blonde. The girls all laughed as the sweet light-haired girl smiled at her group.

"What? It's so bad working in my studio by the beach? How bad can that be?" All the girls laughed good-naturedly as Ein considered the amazing talent shared in this place of exquisite sunsets and fresh seafood. No wonder, many varied artists chose to live here. How could they not receive inspiration from a land of golden skies and blue-green waters? Yes, potters, authors, songwriters and performers, artists, and many other artistic personalities strolled these streets and beaches. Incredibly, this time of year, you never knew who might meander into the dining room for a lazy lunch or sunset dinner. Sometimes, during the Blast on the Bay Songwriter's Festival, the staff was taken aback by the person returning a smile. It sure humbled everyone when a big talent demonstrated that all people are the same. Only some folks are able to express themselves more dramatically. These three gifted young women would undoubtedly be famous someday; no one in Port St. Joe doubted that.

As a few of the servers, including Sam and Allison, stood behind the glass windows looking out onto the porch, a new waitress, Maddie, strode over with a smile. "Wow, look, there's someone famous."

"What? Oh yeah, you mean the good-looking guys in the back? They've been coming here for years. Their parents and grandparents lived here for a very long time. Actually, they still do. Once, those guys spent summers here with their grandparents on Cape San Blas. They are great! Have you attended one of their concerts? They still visit and perform here a great deal of the time," one of the local workers, Ryan, explained as he gazed respectfully at the back table.

"What about the beautiful girls over there with their heads together? What are they typing on their laptop?" Maddie questioned. Simultaneously, the waitresses turned to look at the girls giggling at Table 36 as the three men, they had earlier pointed out, smiled and waved from the back.

"What's wrong with us? We only need one more song. Usually, it's so easy." The tall blonde, Shelley, sounded a little frustrated.

"You do understand how many songs we have already written in three days? We are tired, burned out. We'll get that last one. Let's just relax." The three women thirstily drank from the huge glasses of iced tea placed before them while they glared at the bay for inspiration.

TABLE 36

"Do you all want your regulars?" Sasha, the smiling waitress, felt a little awed at this table of talent. "How's your handsome husband? I went to the concert the other night. He was amazing! Well, you were too. How can you have two different bands and do it all with a family and company?" Sasha studied with awe the talented songwriter who, indeed, did have everything.

"Yes, please, we would all love our regulars. Do *you* have any songs up *your* sleeve? We truly need help here. My family's all fine. Thanks for asking." The lady with the laptop looked hopefully at the waitress wishing for a little inspiration.

"I would love to help you, but I can't write songs. You know, I would love to have your talent. You'll get it. Just relax a little." Quickly, she hurried back to the kitchen, well aware that her group, at Table 36, had a mission and needed to rush.

As the server scurried back to the kitchen, she ran into a familiar face on the little step. The tall man in the black cowboy hat almost walked into her as he waved at the three men seated at the table in the back and the women at Table 36.

"Hold on there little woman. Why the hurry? You need to relax and smell the roses. Is that a song? It would make an awfully good one." His generous smile and humble manner seemed impossible for someone as famous as him. Without speaking, the little waitress gave a big toothy grin before charging back inside. She couldn't wait to describe to the others who had just walked in.

"Guys, look outside. How quickly the sky has changed. Look! Those black clouds are scary. Hear the wind? It is so strong. That old oak tree is scaring me. What if it blows over on us?" The others chuckled at their friend as her dark eyes watched the quickly changing weather out of the windows. These changes frequently happened, here, on the waters by the bay, and no one could possibly guess what horror waited for that big old tree in a little over one year.

A flash of lightning tore from the sky and struck close to the old oak. All the girls jumped as the other diners gasped at this storm, which seemed to have come out of nowhere. "What if our song related falling in love with a storm or a bolt of lightning? What do ya think?" They all bent over the laptop to punch in their ideas.

"Yes, I like it. We can work this out. Come on, ladies, let's write a song!" Again, their heads met at little Table 36, with their exceptional talent energetically working on a new song.

"Have you ever considered the amount of talent in this town? I am amazed, especially at this time of the year around the Annual Songwriter's Festival. Sometimes, it feels as if we live in Nashville. You know?"

The little group of waitresses and waiters observed the special group seated in front of them from the glass windows behind the porch.

8

The months passed quickly in the little town of Port St. Joe, without a sign that someday, very soon, a tragedy would occur that would change everyone's life forever. How could the residents know?

Halloween, in the little town, always presented an opportunity to get creative and design costumes, and dream of winning the prize at the Ghosts of the Coast event that took place on Reid Avenue. That night, goblins haunted the small town, and parents doted over their little ones, with happy smiles radiating from Luke Skywalker and Darth Vader. Music played as the streets were cordoned off from traffic so that young feet could safely trick or treat. These well-mannered young people never played nasty tricks as they hastily filled their bags with snacks enough to last a week.

Inside the Sunset Grill, diners enjoyed another delicious meal of freshly prepared fish and local vegetables. Table 36 proudly welcomed a couple of locals who greeted everyone around them. Mr. and Mrs. Yost happily chatted as they roamed over to the other tables. Finally, they lowered themselves into chairs facing the bay as a glorious sunset of reds and oranges painted the evening sky. They discussed their grandchildren while expressing relief that these children didn't need to trick or treat at the homes of strangers but safely enjoyed treasures gladly provided by local businesses. A wealthy couple made an entrance. They walked with an only daughter, Libby, and her uncle, Sidney. Little did Kayla, the waitress, realize that on this night of terror, a terrible secret was about to be revealed at Table 36.

Kayla approached with a broad smile dressed in a costume that she had designed and sewed herself. All the staff wore disguises, and customers chuckled over the wit of each one. Kayla had worked particularly hard on looking like a beautiful fairy. As a child, she had dreamed of wearing such a lovely outfit on this happy day. Glowing, she felt thankful that everyone seemed to love her little white mesh skirt; she even sported a fairy wand, which she laid aside to take the strangers' orders.

"What a tacky little costume! Libby, I'm glad that you were never into this horrible holiday of making a fool of yourself. Honey, there are places to purchase professional costumes. If you're ever silly enough to do this again, please, take my advice!" The woman laughed as Libby lowered her head. The young lady sighed at her mom's nasty behavior. There wasn't a great deal of joy in this young girl's life. She looked sadly at Kayla, who smiled gaily. The server's life was filled with friends and joyous times. Her family didn't possess much, but they loved their beautiful daughter, unconditionally. The waitress had grown accustomed to insults from wealthy travelers who sometimes viewed the local staff as inferior. Kayla had grown up in this town, whose schools fostered confidence and boldness, especially for young women. As the little fairy, dressed in white, turned to the wealthy daughter, Libby, the sadness of that young girl caused the waitress to stop. Words seemed to pass telepathically between the two young women. Their eyes locked.

Both were strong in their Christian faith. One of them had everything money could buy but had a horrible secret no one knew, an experience that had destroyed her. The other possessed little wealth but owned the world with a golden ribbon due to the love and compassion from those around her. Kayla realized that the sad face, staring at her, needed help, but with what did someone like that rich kid need help? The tall blonde wealthy teenager appeared gorgeously dressed in designer clothes. The fairy princess looked down at her

TABLE 36

own costume that once seemed brilliant and funny but now looked cheap, sad. Libby's teeth shone, bleached to perfection, while the little waitress always tried not to smile too widely so that no one would notice her imperfect teeth. Yes, these two girls were different as night and day, but there was something about Libby that pulled on the heartstrings of her server.

Just as the family placed their orders, a ruckus outside caused a stir among the diners on the porch. Everyone rushed to the windows, pointing and murmuring before running outside toward the bay. Out in the waters, a sailboat had drifted too close to the shore on this gusty day. The day sailor now sat sideways on one of the sandbars. A whole lot of well-meaning sailors yelled what probably wasn't helpful advice to the young captain who looked terrified. Why had he manned the boat alone on such a nasty day?

"That stupid kid, he shouldn't be sailing if he doesn't even know to avoid getting this close and not to sail in this intense wind by himself. I'll go tell him what to do!" said Libby's uncle.

Libby's father, Lee, mumbled something that sounded like "The jerk should mind his own business." He smiled kindly at the server. "He's my wife's brother, Libby's only uncle, and a bit of a bully. I detest him, but he seems to accompany us everywhere, unfortunately." Those were the first kind words the bewildered waitress heard from the strangers at Table 36. At least, Lee hadn't insulted her. Kayla thought that this only act of kindness, speaking to her, not about her, happened because Uncle Sidney and his sister, Harper, had left the room. Finally, Lee followed his wife. All had vacated the table except Libby, who stared intently at Kayla.

"Look, I'm pretty good at reading people. Not perfect, mind you, but usually right in my assessments. Are you trying to tell me something? Your expression looks painful to me. Please tell me that you aren't kidnapped? Do you need my help in some way?" Kayla sputtered in deep concern for the downcast girl.

"Oh, my situation is much worse than being kidnapped. What I'm about to tell you, well . . . I'll deny it if you say anything around them."

She pointed to her family now assembled beneath the large oak tree. "My uncle, Sidney, is a monster. He's molested me since the age of five years. Before you ask me why I haven't told my parents, I have. Of course, I have! They don't believe me. My mother denies this could ever happen in a 'good' family, indeed, not from *her* precious brother. They have me going to an expensive psychiatrist to lessen their guilt. I hate all of them. Honestly, it's only a matter of time until I achieve my goal of obtaining a scholarship to NC State. They have an outstanding veterinarian program. Once I leave for college, I'll never go back to North Carolina. They can shove their hefty trust fund up—well, you get my message. At one time, I dreamed of becoming an accomplished pediatrician, but now, I'll settle for an animal doctor just to have my own life. Anything to escape that monster!"

"I don't understand how this could happen. Didn't you tell a teacher or someone else who could help you through the years?"

"What and leave my cushy home and every convenience in the world? You see, when I was old enough to understand how convoluted and dirty this was, I had endured it for several years. I always believed this behavior was normal. How could I know that none of my friends had to face this abuse? Finally, good old Sidney threatened to kill me if I ever talked. I believed him. Now, he has lost interest in me. I guess I'm too old for his tastes. My hell is almost over, but I'm not finished with him. Since he doesn't bother me anymore, he probably breathes a sigh of relief that no one believed me and he got away with his detestable actions. What he doesn't realize is that I have recorded his little midnight sessions for the last two years. His prestigious world will soon crumble around him and my selfish mother. Can you imagine how it felt knowing that my mother did understand what was happening, but she chose to do nothing in order to protect her wealthy status and creepy brother? I think I hate her more than Sinister Sidney. That's what I once called him in my mind. When I heard his heavy footsteps at night coming to my room, I hid under the bed, but he always jerked me out. Over and over in my mind I

TABLE 36

screamed, 'Sinister Sidney'; it lessened the pain as I pictured a stupid clown with a big red nose."

"Don't look so sad. I'm fine. It's just that I can't wait to get that letter from the university before I spill the dirt on that creep." She smiled, warmly at Kayla.

When Sidney noticed his niece in deep conversation with the stranger at Table 36, he hurried back to his chair. "What's going on here? Libby, you don't even know this girl. Don't speak to her."

"Yes, of course, Uncle Sidney. You're so right." She laughed loudly as did Kayla. The terror on the man's face alerted the girls that he knew. His deepest, nastiest secret lay exposed at the feet of a stranger. He reasoned that this little local could never harm the big North Carolinian tycoon.

Kayla reached her hand out to Libby before she scurried back to deliver the orders to Table 36. "Well, I don't know what that kid in the boat would have done without the helpful instructions of my dearest brother: way to go, Sidney. You probably saved the unambitious life of that silly kid. Libby, do you recall the wonderful summers we all enjoyed in Annapolis? Remember, the *Boardroom*? You know it was the last of Uncle's yachts and the largest."

"Oh yes, Mummy, I do remember the long nights aboard that monstrous boat. I always wondered why you and Uncle Sidney insisted that I be located so far from your stateroom. I mean, there were others much closer to you, darling Mummy."

Harper and Sidney nervously glanced at each other but quickly lowered their eyes. Libby's father, Lee, only joined the family for long weekends during those hot summers years ago since he ran a sprawling corporation. The poor man lived in a world where life was perfect. He felt happy and content, letting his wife make all the decisions at home. His role as CEO of his company consumed him.

Kayla came out of nowhere, as she scurried toward Table 36, with four large glasses of water and lemon slices. The eyes of the two girls met just as that little waitress charged Uncle Sidney. It didn't appear to be an accident as all four glasses of ice-cold water, she had made sure it was freezing, fell onto the lap of the uncle.

"Why did you do that? You little tart! That wasn't an accident!" His vocabulary descended into the gutter as the young mother at the next table covered her little boy's ears. "I'll have your job, you imbecile!"

"Really? You may want to reconsider your threat, *Sidney*. You see, I just recorded my conversation with your niece for backup, should she need it."

"Libby, what's this girl talking about?" The poor dad looked at his wife for understanding. Lee understood something important unfolded before him. What was happening in his perfect world? *What does this stranger know that I don't?*

"We will all leave right now! You cancel our order or eat it yourself. We'll never come back here again." Uncle Sidney appeared terrified and angry as he pranced away.

Libby held her hand in the sign of a phone as Kayla nodded joyfully. She had the card with the phone number of the lovely blonde. Tonight, she would phone her. Kayla planned to be the best of friends to someone who needed kindness.

9

Thanksgiving Day, October of 2017, saw the staff of the Sunset Coastal Grill ready for action! With four seatings scheduled, on this Day of Days, these waiters had to take all the rest they could and be ready to roll. Diners began strolling inside at 11:00 a.m. and continued until 3:30 p.m. The selection waiting for them was "over the moon" as appetizers, soup, and several choices, including ham, turkey, ribs, and seafood, lined the buffet table. This Thanksgiving feast was one of the favorite times in the sunny dining room by the graceful waters of St. Joseph Bay.

About the only thing diners needed to be concerned about was the perfect time to gather their family to begin celebrating! Delicious fragrances wafted through the air on what would be the last Thanksgiving ever prepared and served at Table 36, which now sparkled like a star. Not only local families, stood at the serving stations, but many tourists happily decided that they "must come again next year." That was not going to happen. Already, Mother Nature knew what waited for the community which loved that special dining space.

Several tables had been joined together around Table 36 for the earliest seating. A family of tourists had savored plans for a special Thanksgiving lunch today. They could barely squeeze into the room but had taken the last reservation just to be together at their favorite summer beach retreat. The day had finally arrived as this group celebrated more than Thanksgiving on that joyous day. Harley, Elizabeth, and their four children, as well as two cousins and a niece, were sharing the happy news. After placing drink orders, they hurried to the buffet line with great excitement. Taking time to point at the calamari, the children quickly passed that dish. As they loaded their plates high with juicy treats, it felt almost impossible to contain their joy. Happy news waited, but no one knew what it was. It was a big mystery. Frequently, over the past two days, family members had huddled together, trying to guess what the news might be, but no one felt sure.

As they returned to their places at Table 36, they joined hands and bowed their heads to thank the One who had provided all this great food and a special blessing this year. No one spoke for a very long time as they relished food prepared to perfection and looked forward to long naps upon returning to their hotel rooms. Much too quickly, the plates were emptied as the family headed back to the line for desserts. Mr. Steiner asked the waitress if they might have an extra moment. He realized that the table was reserved for each of the four seatings and didn't want to cause the wait staff any problems. Kindly, Sabrina nodded but glanced nervously at the owner, who had asked them to clean the table quickly for waiting diners.

Rushing to choose his sweet selections, Harley almost ran into the owner who smiled at him. She knew about this table because she had personally made this reservation a little earlier in the week. When Mr. Steiner explained the good news, he'd waited to share with his family, the owner, Patti, had wiped a tear from her eye and decided she must be there early to meet this special group.

"Okay, family, I know you must wonder why I made such a big deal about gathering you all here for Thanksgiving. We usually meet here in June, and we all surely hope to keep our tradition next summer, but today, I wanted to share *my* news with you. You may suspect what I'm about to share, but you may be wrong. You see, I haven't even shared this with my wife.

"Elizabeth, my love, you have been faithful and loving to me for over forty years. We all thought this would be my last Thanksgiving.

TABLE 36

As you are well aware, I fought colon cancer for over two years. You all know that after we celebrated two summers ago the ugly beast raised his hateful head once again. This past year, my hell continued." The family lowered their heads, remembering Harley's heroic fight against the evil of cancer.

"Anyway, I see our waitress looking a little stressed. I believe that her next group of diners wait behind her, there, in the hall. Family, I received the best news of my life two weeks ago. I am cured again. It is hard for me to believe that I've been given another chance to enjoy time on this earth and look into your eyes for another period. God is so good. Our prayers are answered! We'll all meet here, again, this June, as in years past. Our time will not be cut short."

Tears of joy silently fell. Elizabeth grabbed his hand. Oh, how she had prayed that this might be the good news he had hinted at, but he also had mentioned buying a beach house for the family to continue to enjoy after his death. His announcement of being able to share more time with them was the best news he could have given them.

Sabrina sighed as she turned back to check on the family waiting for Table 36. Although she understood this important family meeting, she hated to see another family become upset because their reservations weren't being honored punctually. Finally, the group rose from the tables with gigantic smiles and full stomachs. Life was good, here, in Port St. Joe.

What the small band couldn't know was that they would not be meeting ever again at this place on bright sunny days with breathtaking purple sunsets, enjoying great food at Table 36. Even though they might, once again, congregate inside their favorite rental unit to enjoy the month of June, which they had enjoyed together for ten years, it wouldn't be the same ever again. Things were about to change in this coastal town of Tupelo honey and purple azaleas. Life, as they all knew and loved, was about to change forever. Unfortunately, the day hell broke loose was around the corner.

10

The list of diners who waited all year for the scrumptious meal at Thanksgiving had grown each year. Adding extra seats to accommodate those additional reservations was easy to accomplish. This action wasn't possible for New Year's Eve. The partiers at this once a year event were many. Even gaining entrance to the lively scene required reservations made in advance as locals and "snow birds" rushed in for their table. One thing that made this event special was that Port St. Joe fell into the EST zone while neighboring Mexico Beach was in the CST zone. This small fact made celebrating New Year's Eve twice as good. Revelers celebrated the New Year with fireworks in Port St. Joe at 10:00 p.m. It was then possible to catch a shuttle (there were nine of them) and journey the few miles to neighboring beaches and watch the extravaganza once again at midnight CST. This little fact made celebrating more fun and was a massive draw for tourists to Port St. Joe and Mexico Beach.

Dinner at Sunset Grill on this night of double celebrating began at 5:00 p.m. and continued until well after midnight. The special menu pleased even the most discriminating palettes as many revelers dressed in gay apparel to usher in the new year.

"Watch your step, please." Lisa was dressed in her sexiest dress to welcome the eager diners for an extraordinary celebration. She beamed at the familiar couple who arrived early for the first seating.

TABLE 36

They were locals. Quietly, the striking couple followed her. The restaurant shone as each table stood uniquely decorated with party whistles and hats as well as candies and take away tidbits. Shining colors of red and purple hung from the ceilings. Lisa escorted the solemn couple to Table 36 and then rushed away to seat the next group.

"You look exceptionally beautiful tonight, darling. I love that red dress. Not many women could pull that off, but you do. You are amazing." Henry smiled sadly at his wife, Clarice. His words sounded robotic, expected. Great pain registered in his hazel eyes. Sadly, he lowered his head.

Clarice didn't smile; instead, she gazed wearily around the room. *Everyone* shone tonight. Her mind tried to recall how many New Year's Eve dinners they had enjoyed here, at this little table, but there were too many to remember. In their youth, they had celebrated in the St. Joe Room at a larger table. Through the years, friends had died or moved away. Now, it was just the two of them, alone, once again.

Silently, they drank the champagne, which accompanied their meal. It wasn't especially great, but life no longer held the glow or expectation of the extraordinary. Ordinary was the bar; it never changed. Clarice dreaded tonight. How many times had she tried to find a way to break the news to her husband of forty-five years that it was over between them? A new love had entered her life totally as a surprise. In fact, it was Henry's fault that she had met the tall younger man with intense dark blue eyes and jet-black hair. Never, had the two expected to fall in love.

"Henry, you've got to be kidding me. A gym membership at my age? Won't I look foolish? You know, like one of those old gals who try to appear young? Maybe, I can get a refund. That's a significant amount to throw away."

He had coaxed her into joining the small gym located on Reid Avenue by reminding her how young she already appeared. It was true. Whenever she was forced to tell her age, everyone refused to believe she was so old. Yes, she did continue to exercise and eat sparingly.

Over a few days, she had convinced herself that she deserved time alone to work on maintaining her weight. *Maybe, my husband's idea wasn't so fanciful?*

Reluctantly, she had begun to attend a morning session at the gym. At first, she had felt out of place, but she had forced herself to keep going. Eventually, the older woman loved it! There, time just seemed to evaporate. Each day, she desired to feel the effect of the endorphins that were released as she worked away the extra pounds. It was a drug, driving her to desire more and more. Soon, she felt grateful to her husband for this gift, which created so much joy. Her smile returned as the fulfilled wife loved life again.

Then, this extremely handsome younger man had begun to hang around her. He seemed harmless and fun. They began to work out together, and her workout became more enjoyable. Jackson's silly remarks kept her laughing. Before long, Clarice looked forward to seeing him more than exercising.

Her choice in exercise attire changed. Brighter colors now appealed to her instead of the drab colors of the past. A little dip to the top didn't really reveal that much, she told herself. If the leotards were tighter, they seemed to hold that flab around the middle a little closer. It felt silly wearing makeup to workout but why not look good, she tortured herself with questions. Jackson complimented her on her choice of sexier outfits. His flattery seemed what she needed in her boring life. After all these years with Henry, things felt a little stale.

One rainy day, as she prepared to leave the gym, Jackson begged her to join him for a quick bite down the street. *Why not?* she had asked herself. After all, her husband always ate out after *his* daily golf game. He wouldn't return home for two more hours.

Their first lunch was innocent and quick. Clarice felt on edge that she would see a close friend at any moment, but soon she realized that there were no longer any friends. Years of reclusive living had stripped her of social connections. Being with Jackson was fun. There wasn't any reason to feel guilty. Didn't Henry come home

TABLE 36

laughing each day with hysterical tales of *his* friends? Why shouldn't she live a little? Although she never shared her antics at lunch with her husband.

Their lunches soon became the high point of her life as they switched from the sandwich place to the Mexican restaurant at Pepper's. There, they enjoyed a margarita as they laughed away the hour. One hour became two as one margarita became another. Jackson began to sit beside her instead of across the table. His touch electrified the older woman. Often, she asked herself what a successful younger man could see in her? Eventually, she posed the question that tormented her during long nights, as she listened to the loud snores of her husband. They didn't usually bother her, but lately, everything Henry did seemed to grate on her.

"You've got to be kidding, right? You're asking me what I see in you? That's what I ask myself each night. *What does Clarice possibly see in me?* Your husband, Henry, is well known and respected in the area. I often wondered why you guys never socialized. I've always been attracted to you, Clarice, and desired to meet you. When I saw you that first day at the gym, I almost did a flip. It was never my intention to fall in love with you."

There, he had said *the* word. Tears flooded the brown eyes of the dark-haired beauty who now visited the salon each month for coloring and manicures. Those red toenails sparkled at her each night as she applied lotion. *For what?* she had asked herself. Henry was not interested in her looks.

"Clarice, I love you for many reasons besides your incredible beauty. The way you laugh and the kindness you show strangers. Do you have any idea how proud I would be to escort you through life together? I long for *our* life together. Do you understand? My desires aren't about wild sex or tawdry nights. I want to share the rest of my time on this earth with *you*. Think about it, will you? Can you leave him?"

Clarice laughed gaily at his silly comments. Sometimes, his youth surprised her. *What a ridiculous statement*; of course, she would never leave her husband, but the seed was sown. Hours without seeing

Jackson seemed forever. Around her husband, she became irritable and short. All day she longed to touch Jackson's face or hold his hand. Nothing more intimate than that had occurred between the two. Truth be told, she wanted to spend the night with the younger man but would never raise that proposition, even though each night was filled with desire to feel him beside her in the lonely cold room. One year after the innocent present for a membership to the local gym, she was about to make the hardest decision of her life. *How will I face each day without my best friend?* Quickly, a voice in her head whispered, *You'll have Jackson.* She loved both of them.

What needed be done couldn't happen. Clarice tried to broach the subject of leaving her husband, but his familiar smile and the way he clasped her hand stopped her from speaking. Her hands began to shake, and her left eye twitched. "What's wrong, my darling? You look so tense. Here we are celebrating the end of another year, but you hardly speak. I know you, Clarice. What's wrong?" Henry watched his love as tears stained her cheeks. She tried to talk but appeared unable. Unbeknown to his wife, Henry flicked tears from his own eyes. What he must now do was the most challenging and demanding action of *his* life.

"Okay, I'll do this for you, Clarice. I came to the gym early one day. I cut my golf game short so that I could take you to lunch. I had noticed the change in your appearance, the loss of weight and sexy looks. Naturally, I was curious. When I saw the younger man, I knew. It devastated me. I thought that I might die for the longest time. Maybe, if I had confronted you, at that point, I may have prevented your relationship from growing, but I didn't want to if you were unhappy. You see, I love you *that* much. Your life is precious to me. More than any person on this earth, I love you. What's the old cliché? If you love someone, set them free. If they don't come back, they never really loved you. Something like that, I think. Anyway, that's what we're doing tonight. Clarice, I'm gonna set you free. You do what you must. I'll tell you this, if you're ever unhappy, you come on home. I know that you won't.

TABLE 36

"One of my golf buddies saw you and the young man enjoying a few margaritas at lunch a few weeks ago. I also went there the next day. I even stood about two feet from your table, but you only had eyes for your new love. When I saw the way you looked at him, I realized that you never looked at me like that over the forty years of our marriage. I determined, on that day, that I must cut the cord. What do you desire I do? Want to go home with me or should I get a hotel room until our union is severed?"

The stunned waitress, who couldn't help but hear all this as she speedily cleaned the next table, covered her eyes when she hurried from the scene. Lisa had served these folks now for thirteen years. They were among her favorite diners. *How can this happen?* Her heart broke for the kind man who always overtipped.

Maybe this heartbreaking scene was the backdrop for the pain that waited for the two little towns of Port St. Joe and Mexico Beach. The lives of all the residents were also about to change. Great pain awaited them just like that of divorce. Floridians would lose what they loved and be forced to begin a new life, just like poor Henry. The sad thing was that, as this couple faced the hardest moments of their many years together, they would also be forced to lose all they loved.

They must soon cope with another unwanted hardship. During the next months, whatever personal hell innocents endured, they would be saddled with more heartbreak from something else unexpected. As blameless folks celebrated a new year, they couldn't know that the next year, their favorite dining spot wouldn't exist as hell sneered around the corner.

11

Sweet January of 2018 began as usual. New Year resolutions flooded the minds of well-meaning, hardworking Gulf and Bay County residents. The bright fireworks from the beaches celebrating a brand-new year passed. It was time to get back to daily schedules: braces for the kids, and all the political news. So many decisions and problems faced young families as they tried to better their lives and provide for those they loved. Not much time was spent on worrying about what might happen this year.

The next big day was Valentine's Day as couples looked forward to spending much-needed time together. The children were lovingly looked after by grandparents or baby sitters as Mom and Dad enjoyed a great meal with maybe a bottle of wine and flowers. Each couple scheduled their time together with hopes of a little romance.

The Sunset Coastal Grill always planned a special meal with yummy desserts to induce the feeling of "letting go and enjoying these precious hours together." Most of the large tables were broken down and prepared for couples. Table 36 was reserved all night—the beloved space represented for many a place where life made sense with a warm welcome from their favorite servers.

Gloria and Hal Robinson held hands as they took a deep breath. Their new baby, Sally, was safely tucked in the crib at home under the watchful eye of Hal's mother. "Watch your step, please. We don't

TABLE 36

want any broken bones on the night of love." They laughed at the silly warning of the hostess as they stepped with care off the little step.

Waiting on Table 36 was a single rose in a small crystal vase. There was also a large box of chocolates, which Hal didn't have time to wrap, but had dropped off the items at the restaurant before hurrying to pick up his wife.

"What, chocolates *and* my favorite yellow rose? How did I get such a catch? You know, honey, all the girls in school hated me when we started dating. They all said you would never be in the dating pool again after we met. It seems they were right!" She smiled, lovingly at her handsome husband.

Hal beamed at the most beautiful girl at Port St. Joe High School. Even back then, when he had passed her in the halls, he had found it difficult to breathe. Now, after college and marriage, he loved Gloria even more, if possible.

Anna, the waitress, laughed softly. "She's so right, Hal. I was just one of the crew who fell madly in love with you way back then." She fluttered her eyelashes for effect. Everyone laughed gaily at the antics of the spunky waitress. Her wit was notoriously funny.

Hal took the hand of the blonde beauty facing him. "You know, Gloria, I think, I now love you more than ever before. How can that be possible? After all this time and the birth of our first child, you continue to take my breath. God sure knew what he was doing when he placed us together."

The young woman looked into the brown eyes that she loved more than any other. Her memories returned to high school and the terror she had faced each day. At that time, she didn't know about anxiety attacks or that they even existed. Gloria *did* realize that social interactions terrified her. *I guess everyone feels this way*, she often chided herself.

Gloria had forced herself to participate in many clubs and even cheerleading, which caused great trepidation in her. When Hal had approached, one day in the hall, with his casual demeanor and gorgeous smile, something had melted inside her. When she walked beside him, or even if he only waited in the bleachers, a new calmness overtook her. This newfound peace bolstered her confidence, allowing her to accomplish so much more with her life. She doubted if she would have ever attempted applying to college if he hadn't threatened that he wouldn't go without her. Yes, the man before her represented more than just the love of her life; he was her foundation.

As they continued to hold hands and gaze into each other's eyes, the waitresses lined up, once again, behind the windows of the porch. Each of the women longed to find what this couple seemed to possess. *Why did some people have everything?* No words passed as the servers continued to dream of finding someone as genuine as Hal, just as each doubted it could happen to them.

Behind Hal's head, the sky filled with pink, blue, and purple swaths of bright, intense color. It was as though God had said, "I'm with you, dear children of Port St. Joe. Never forget or doubt my love for you. Sometimes, I must let terrible things happen to my beloved, but I'll never leave or forsake you. Please, never forget that." God must have shed a tear for what waited.

12

When March rolled onto the calendar, in the town of Port St. Joe, in 2018, something exceptional happened on Cape San Blas. A group of artists arrived each year around the end of that month. The Forgotten Coast welcomed internationally acclaimed artists each year. This year was no exception. The artists gladly accepted invitations to enjoy the beauty of nature and historic architecture as they practiced what they loved, Plein air art. For thirteen years, the gracious ladies of Cape San Blas opened hearts, homes, as well as wallets, to a group containing extraordinary expertise. This *Great Paint Out* rated as one of the most prestigious art events in the world. The competition lasted for ten days. Each year, the number of artists varied but was usually around twenty. Homes of residents were spruced up as all sorts of much-needed repairs were finally accomplished, often at great expense, to the cheers of the wives and groans of the husbands.

Locals would witness easels sat by the side of the road as talented artisans captured scenes of local egrets, pelicans, and other birds as well as just the beauty of the changing waters. Sunsets wowed the crowd. Each morning, the beauty of a new sunrise demonstrated God's love for this earth.

Many painters chose to capture the historic beauty of an ancient church or maybe a brick restaurant that had begun to sag. History ran deep in old Port St. Joe and the surrounding counties. Even the cemetery, at Old St. Joseph, stirred the interest of many as they considered the lost city of this area. Only a few remaining brick tombs and tombstones marked the graves of those who perished long ago. There exists no exact count of the bodies harbored in mass graves. Most were buried in 1841 after a disastrous yellow fever epidemic swept through the frontier area. About six thousand residents called this home after the yellow fever epidemic, but the deadly hurricane reduced the number of living to only five hundred in the little coastal town. The city then promised a "healthy climate" and boasted of fresh air sweeping in from the sea and breezes that blew off the gulf and bay. Many ran from the humidity and baking temperatures of landlocked sites only to later perish in the coastal town. Yes, the fresh air had "swept in from the sea," but the intensity of that wind could never have been expected.

There existed a troubling history, here, beloved as the town was, but regardless of the stories of yellow fever, ghosts, and terrible storms, residents who called this place home refused to abandon it. They loved those beaches of white, as they looked forward each evening to share a cocktail by the gentle sea breeze from the gulf, in a special land where great turtles chose to deposit their eggs.

During this ten-day event, all sorts of galas and competitions whetted the appetite of confident art designers who boasted of receiving hefty prices for their work. Admirers of breathtaking paintings waited anxiously for the flocks of strangers with incredible talent to invade their humble homes. Not only artists but fans of each one of them often followed. Restaurants filled at lunch and dinner as these strangers laughed with new friends over the mishaps of the day. There were always plenty of those.

Sunset Coastal Grill received its share of reservations from the hosts and guests. Table 36, remained reserved for the ten days of their soirée. "Watch your step." Vicky gently turned to the older artist who excitedly talked with her hostess. Maggie Eckerd always opened her home to a gifted stranger. Each year's talent hung proudly on her

TABLE 36

walls, as she had previously hosted seven of these painters through the past years. Maggie loved to show her friends the gifts given to her for sharing room and meals with strangers. All these presents were her reward for willingly opening her home to unknowns.

Laughing uncontrollably at a funny comment from her artist guest this year, Liza Comings, Maggie failed to hear the warning from Vicky as she waved to a neighbor also treating *her* guest to lunch. Just as Liza began to sit at Table 36, Maggie missed her step. The drop wasn't much. It was only one small step but enough to turn the hostess's ankle and cause severe bruising and pain.

All laughter stopped as everyone hurried to assist the dining room hostess in lifting the fallen lady. Maggie tried to appear brave as she chuckled over her clumsiness, but the damaged area on her left leg had already begun to swell and change color. The pain increased with each minute.

"Oh, poo, I hate this. Mostly, I regret having to miss the final party at Indian Pass. Do you know how much I love *that* event? Well, poo, I guess, my activities will be squelched for the duration of your visit. I truly apologize, Liza."

Joan Greene dashed to the side of the injured lady. "Don't call it over yet. I have a walker, which you can use. We'll get you up those stairs on the last night. Shucks, we'll make sure you don't miss a single event." She smiled sweetly as she lifted the tea towel covering the raised foot and a bluish-green ankle. The site of injury didn't look right.

"Really, that would be great! Thank you." Maggie breathed a sigh of relief. She loved the social scene in the area.

"Mrs. Eckerd, I want you to know that my husband and I have a van that we never use. Maybe your artist friend can drive *you*, so that you can keep your foot elevated, as you attend different functions. We never use the older vehicle anymore after we got our new SUV. We'll drop it by your house tomorrow."

"Well, Maggie, I want you to know that several of us ladies have already planned meals for the next ten days. You don't need to worry

about how to feed your husband or guest. We've got ya covered."
Justine Sears beamed with pride at her quick response. Justine was
the local gourmet cook. Everyone loved to receive an invitation to
dinner from her.

Liza Cummings shook her head in disbelief. "Wow! Where I come
from, you wouldn't have received a single offer for help. You'd be on
your own. Can I move here?"

Maggie glowed with gratitude for this special place, which loved
to encourage and help as needed. "You bet you can! Welcome to Port
St. Joe, Liza!" The sunshine streamed in through the windows and
bounced off the shiny surface of little Table 36.

13

As the weather continued to warm, another exceptional month smiled on the little town. The blessed month of May welcomed everyone in the area with bright sunny mornings and quick afternoon showers, which only made the blooming flowers more brilliant. Glorious purple and pink azalea blooms that thrilled horticulturists as did flowering shrubs of pink and white English hawthorn.

Pale pudgy bodies, hiding indoors for months, ventured into the bright sunshine with generous applications of sunscreen. Heavy residents began to pump bikes on the many trails crisscrossing the town. Gardeners made new plans for showcasing brightly colored cascades of flowers spilling over newly painted fences. Bird feeders received a thorough washing as hummingbirds were bid "Welcome home."

The local hardware store filled with husbands grumbling over the lengthy "honey-do" list. "Do you see the list my wife gave me this year? I won't be able to fish for two months. Shoot, I'll probably miss the red snapper season this year! Her list grows each year. What's a husband to do?" Similar complaints echoed around the cash register as the owner smiled. His new house still needed work, so he understood the complaints about the "infamous list."

Table 36 boasted a new brass flower holder with a fresh pink azalea bloom from someone's garden. Residents loved to provide flowers for the tables of their neighbors and friends especially at little Table 36. New faces pranced into the restaurant because this was the weekend for the historic *Apalachicola Home and Garden Tour,* which occurred each first weekend in May. Even though Apalachicola was located twenty-eight miles from Port St. Joe, many visitors flocked to see *this* town and the beach at Cape San Blas. Apalachicola couldn't boast of a gorgeous beach of sugary white sand.

The Tour of Homes received sponsorship from the Trinity Episcopal Church as it vouched for the authenticity of the small coastal town, which indeed presented visitors with eternal charm and mouth-watering food. For twenty-six years, this event packed the area and filled the restaurants, as lovers of historic homes flocked to enjoy the real deal. The tour allowed patrons to stroll the grounds without fussy guides, but several greeters waited in each abode to answer questions and provide assistance as needed. A reception and meal were also offered. All the proceeds were used for maintaining the historic church.

As with every event, Table 36 waited for patrons with reservations to fill the four chairs surrounding it. Amazingly, it was occupied by exciting people with tales of travels from all over the world. On this day, a fresh purple azalea glowed from the shining brass holder at the center of the table. An older couple slowly approached escorted by their only son. They didn't speak but nodded at the hostess who warned them about the first step.

"You know, I'm thrilled that we could open our home again. How many times has it been featured in the tour over these many years? I can't remember." Mrs. Deaton carefully placed her napkin on her lap as she rubbed her ruby lips together. It was hard to eat anymore without dropping crumbs. Still, she tried to remain meticulous.

Her son, Ron, shook his head. "Gee, Mom, you and Dad have done this every few years since I can remember." This local family treasured their historic Greek Revival home, which had been in the family since 1869. Most of the homes in Apalachicola were of the Queen Anne style dominating the neighboring town. The builders, then, as now, desired a view of the bay, so the older homes sat on the

TABLE 36

most expensive lots facing the water, leaving few waterfront sites for modern buildings. Many large structures showcased hipped, cabled, and cross-gabled roofs.

"You know, Mary Neil, I think more people attend the event each year. Aren't you getting tired of letting these strangers roam through our place? Let some of those newer folks share the joy, so to speak," said Mr. Deaton, looking at his son, while realizing that suggestion would not be well received.

Ron covered his mouth as he tried not to laugh at the kindest man in the world. Les, his father, always treated his mother with such love and respect. Being their son was the easiest assignment he could have been given. His mother shook her silver curls, for Mary Neil's hair remained full and lustrous in spite of age. "No way, I'm proud of the house your family gave to us so long ago. We must continue to welcome others into our life; let's not be selfish, Les. We've done it all these many years without incident. Why stop now? You do realize how many folks love our home?" Her smile radiated from a kind heart.

Once again, the waitresses lined up at the windows behind the porch watching interactions between lunchtime diners. They knew the older couple, at their favorite table, could trace their lineage back to the beginning of the area.

"Have you ever been inside their home? I have. It was on the last tour of homes when they showed, I think out of all the homes, over there." She pointed in the direction of Apalachicola. A healthy sense of competition remained between *that* city and Port St. Joe. "Well, their place is the prettiest. Could that have been one of the houses that was originally here, in Port St. Joe? I still get angry that they carried some of *our* homes away." Sasha lowered her head.

Bette chimed in, "I don't know. Always, when I visit there, I wonder which houses they stole." The group of women scoffed at her remark.

"They didn't steal them; you know that, right?" Judith wasn't sure but felt confident that the houses weren't hijacked.

Bette carried the dishes of fragrant seafood to Table 36 with pride, where she placed them perfectly before the small family, who nodded again and offered thanks to God. As the waitress walked away, she pondered the long and sometimes rocky history between the two neighboring cities. Later, after the catastrophic event that rocked Port St. Joe, she would often ponder the similarities between the storms of 1844 and 2018 when Apalachicola was, once again, barely touched.

14

Featuring different events presented a challenge for each tourist town. Visitors loved to congregate in small coastal historic towns along the eastern coast. Competition for attention was intense. A new event, recently added in Port St. Joe, was the June Forgotten Coast Turtle Festival. George Core Park would welcome locals and guests on the last Sunday of June for a new event. Attendees continued to increase as word spread. *Who doesn't love turtles?* The fact that so many turtles lay eggs on the beach of Cape San Bas was another particular draw for Gulf County. So many unusual sites and events lured guests to this special place. Families enjoyed bringing their children to receive instruction on environmental concerns given by the experts who explained things in a way kids understood. Local vendors displayed all sorts of interesting wares for purchase while different stations impressed on young minds the need for clean beaches and not interfering with the flow of nature. The love for turtles in Gulf County rapidly became apparent to anyone visiting the area from signs standing on the Cape San Blas highways and beaches. Small people left this special place with an understanding of the role they must assume if these tiny creatures were to thrive.

"Please, watch your step!" Vicky always felt nervous when small children first entered the bright porch. Their eyes automatically drifted to the streaming sun, blue waters, and the large oak tree outside.

The swaying Palm Tree fronds presented another distraction to their little minds, while their tiny steps attempted to reach their table safely. Little voices squealed with delight at the bright light that reflected off pastel walls. This family arrived for dinner just as the sun began to set. Immediately, the little ones stopped in the middle of the aisle to stare at the gorgeous colors streaming across the sky and the quick dropping of the vast red ball below the horizon. After everyone was safely seated, Ein turned to assist another group.

"So, Becky, how did you like the turtle lady?" the father, Paul, asked his young daughter because he was enamored with the tall woman who had shared interesting facts with them earlier. His wife, Ginger, tapped his arm with a quick smile.

"I liked her. She is so pretty, Dad."

"She certainly is." Paul laughed gleefully while his wife studied the menu.

"Can we come back next month for the Fourth, honey? Remember how brilliant the fireworks are here? It's my favorite place to celebrate our patriotism." Ginger waited for his reply.

"You're darn right. If I get to see that turtle lady." The couple hugged laughing as the children talked about the turtles. Happily, they recited facts they had just learned.

"Dad, can we watch the baby turtles hatch?" Jordan, their six-year-old, overturned his chair without incident. Vicky rushed to help before their waiter knew of the mishap.

"Sweetie, it's not that easy. We don't know precisely when the babies may decide to come. Dad and I would love to do that someday. The season stretches from May through October so if we return in July, maybe?" She smiled at the funny way in which the wife enticed her husband to return next month for the fireworks.

"If we return next year, at the beginning of the season, we may even watch the large mothers crawl to their nests to lay eggs. Wouldn't that be fun?" The eyes of both kids told her how exciting this sounded to them.

TABLE 36

"You know, there are hundreds of nests with eggs. Many of them are loggerheads, which are an endangered species. Do you remember what the turtle lady told us about those extraordinary creatures?"

The kids quickly lost interest as the conversation became technical. "I liked the turtle lady because her skin is really dark, and so is her hair."

Jordan had recovered from his tumble.

"Yes, I noticed that too, Jordan."

"Give it up, Paul. You're beginning to annoy me. We all agree that the turtle lady is charming." He flicked a piece of lemon from Ginger's chin as he winked.

"Hey, Dad, why did you knock down that cool sandcastle? I liked it." Jordan looked quizzically at his dad.

"Don't you remember what the, um, that lady said?" He smiled innocently at his wife.

"I'm not sure. What did the turtle lady say?"

"She said when people dig holes in the sand or build obstacles like sandcastles, they can prevent the mother from safely arriving at her nest. Sometimes, the mother or baby may fall into a hole and never reach safety. We've got to help them, Jordan. I felt sad to destroy someone's handiwork, but Cape San Blas is a special place and needs all of us to teach others about the sea oats and the turtles, right?"

Ginger listened intently to the wise words of her husband, happy that he'd stopped discussing the turtle lady. The waitress asked for their orders as darkness fell over a place where turtles and all nature were loved.

15

"Plenty of places offer fantastic fireworks to lure tourists, but the magic of Port St. Joe is that there are many areas where such firework displays can be enjoyed. Fireworks explode into the sky at the marina as well as all over Cape San Blas Beach. Mexico Beach offers the same spectacle. Maybe, you can witness it all. One thing's for sure: there never will be a shortage of spectacular lights flooding the skies in the Gulf and Bay Counties. Your family chose the best place to witness breathtaking fireworks."

The sheriff briskly strolled into Sunset Coastal for his reserved table, 36, after talking briefly with a group of tourists about the fireworks that evening. Already, there was magic in the air as people excitedly made plans for that evening's Fourth of July celebrations. He was meeting one of his deputies for lunch. A new guy had just joined the force; tonight's celebrations would provide a challenge for all the patrols. So many things could go wrong in a town located by the water.

Everyone worried about boating accidents, drownings, and drunk drivers. Plus, they were always concerned about theft and fights. Alcohol usually seemed to fan the flames of all this. Although crime in their little town remained low, with mostly property cases, one never knew what waited on any particular night. Law enforcement had to be ready for anything, so they had just added a new guy, Ramond.

TABLE 36

"Okay, Sheriff, watch your step." Vicky turned to smile at her friend. It always thrilled her to be able to order this big man around. He laughed generously. The town loved their sheriff.

"What, the new guy isn't here yet, and I'm a little late? Just bring me my usual. He's late, and I don't have time to wait for him." The sheriff began to walk toward the men's room when the new deputy sauntered inside.

"Wow, what a view! Do you dine here often, Sheriff?"

His superior was already stressed with the long night waiting for him. He didn't need to hand-feed a person late for his first day. Rolling his eyes, he strode away but returned quickly. There was just something about this place that could soothe the most tired, stressed person. The experienced law enforcer needed to relax a moment, catch his breath, and enjoy his job because he did love it.

The waitresses stood behind the glass, again, observing the two men. It was a slow time at lunch today. Tonight would be the time the crowd flooded the restaurant before the fireworks began. Softly, the women staff of Sunset chatted among themselves about how important it was to have an excellent police and sheriff team.

"We really do have the best." One of the ladies offered. "Our police crew is just as dedicated as the county staff."

"I'm glad that everyone in our town respects and reveres these men. Do you realize how blessed we are just living here in a small town where there's mostly peace?"

Life happened as always on this lazy Fourth of July. The yearly fireworks went off as smoothly as usual, presenting no problems.

In only a little over three months, the most significant problem Gulf and Bay Counties ever faced would assail them. Each member of the Police and Sheriff Departments would be needed. Their kind acts would never be forgotten.

16

The dog days of summer, July 3–August 11, considered the hottest time of the year passed calmly. It would surprise most people to find *that* name doesn't derive from the fact that the weather outside isn't fit for a dog but rather that it refers to the time the sun shares the same part of the sky with Sirius, the brightest star visible from any location on earth. Also known as the Dog Star, Sirius is part of the constellation Canis Major, also called, the Greater Dog. Hence, the expression "dog days of summer." The dog days, mark the twenty days before and after Sirius aligns with the Sun. Actually, the intense heat is due to the tilting of the earth and not this alignment. Also, in late August, the waters of the Atlantic are at their warmest. No one can argue that the final days of summer are usually pretty miserable.

Finally, August 2018 ended, but dreaded September greeted the townspeople like it or not. Those who resided on the beach looked at the sky in the hope that there would be no hurricane that season. Usually, hurricane season peaked during late August till the end of September with around September 10 considered the climatological peak of activity. Although no one wanted summer to end, a feeling of relief permeated coastal towns lining the Atlantic seaboard once the "dreaded month" passed. Although there were warnings about the possibility of these "monsters from the sea" from June 1 till November 30, for most areas in the Atlantic, September was the marker.

TABLE 36

Imagine the relief everyone in the two towns felt as they sighed deeply with another threat to life removed. Life was hard enough, for most people, without the trauma of annihilation, these storms wreaked. Folks ventured outside with the passing of August and September and the sweltering weather. They relaxed, removing storm shutters and feeling a sense of freedom from an attacker blowing in from the gulf.

October holds an endearing place in the very soul of coastal homeowners. Happy beachgoers smile as they savor the beauty they love without being forced to swat flies and dodge the heat. To those who treasure the shoreside life, this is one of the best months!

Most people weren't even aware that on October 2, 2018, the National Hurricane Center began monitoring an area of low pressure over the southwestern Caribbean Sea. *So what? These things occur all summer long. You can't be upset about every low-pressure area reported. There's always a low-pressure area somewhere that needs watching. No big deal, cyclone season's almost over, right?*

At that same time, that area in the Caribbean Sea experienced a burst of convection possibly associated with a tropical wave. This strengthened as it drifted northward and then westward toward the Yucatán Peninsula. On October 6, weather reports stated that the system still wasn't well organized, so few took it as anything serious. Just the same, most folks on the Panhandle began to watch this possible threat. On the morning of October 7, a radar center in Belize announced the low pressure had become a tropical depression, but it had taken an entire week to strengthen to that level. Still, it now had everyone's attention. Later, that same day, at noon, the depression was referred to as Tropical Storm Michael. The storm continued strengthening, and on October 8 it gained the title Hurricane Michael. Now, people got nervous.

The growing hurricane charged into the Yucatán Peninsula, located in the Gulf of Mexico, as it clipped the western end of Cuba. At this point, it had a Category 2 status. While Floridians, especially in the Panhandle, watched this monster move toward them, most were shocked. It was too late in the year for this region to experience hurricanes or so they thought. Traveling over the gulf, this freak gained momentum as it attained Category 5 status just before hitting Mexico Beach with maximum sustained winds of 160 mph at 2:00 p.m. on October 10, 2018. Michael rated as the first storm *ever* to reach this intensity and land in the Florida Panhandle. Residents were stunned.

Strangely, Michael could maintain this Category 5 intensity only for one hour once it touched land. It quickly diminished while blowing over the inner southeastern United States. Twelve hours after making landfall the once most intense-rated storm was again labeled a tropical storm. However, Michael's fury had already destroyed large sections of the Gulf and Bay Counties. Humans and animals lay crushed and property was destroyed. What remained standing from the assault of the brute would never be the same again.

The area resembled a war zone. Those who decided to "ride out the storm," for whatever reason, suffered PTSD; some would never recover from the anxiousness that gripped them. Frequently, they stared at the heavens wondering, *What might happen today.* Families were often forced to live apart as members searched for work in other areas. Those who evacuated returned in shock at what waited to greet them. It wasn't a greeting but a nightmare that would continue for many residents even a year later.

Sunset Coastal Grill, which once stood proudly on the Gulf of Mexico, was ripped apart. The part of the building facing the water, where golden scenes welcomed so many, was destroyed beyond recognition. The beloved sunny porch was torn entirely from its foundation. Furniture, lifted from the once happy room, was swept into the angry waters never to be seen. *What happened to the little evergreen tree with the funky decorations?* No one knows. Surprisingly, the two old oak trees, which weren't healthy-looking, to begin with, remained barely changed from the relentless assault. The dark green palms still swayed gently in the wind as though waiting for the crowds of diners to return. Diners longed to return, to enjoy life as in the past, but that was never to be.

TABLE 36

The resilience of the human spirit is remarkable. In less than a year, homes in the area were rebuilt; smiles radiated as they did before the monster shook the familiar world of those who lived along the coast. Neighborhood churches, although severely damaged or totally destroyed, continued to fill with humble thanksgiving for allowing residents a second chance. The story here is not unique. There are so many hurricane victims who have tales of survival to tell, but what we see here is a community that didn't beg for help. These proud people rolled up their sleeves as they helped neighbors recover. The outpouring of love, from people and organizations from all over the world, touched battered hearts as strangers made broken lives bearable. Thank you to all who took time from their busy lives to help our residents.

Yes, Sunset Grill is gone. It will never return, or if it does, it couldn't be the same, but the grins in the streets are the same. The love for life and God can never be taken away as *#Port St. Joe Strong* radiates from eyes that understand loss and pain.

17

As Michael completed its assault on Port St. Joe and Mexico Beach, many of the local churches were reduced to rubble. Church steeples sprawled on the ground for months as the old brick landmarks no longer greeted residents. Eyes appeared swollen when citizens passed by, even though smiles still abounded in the streets. The agony of the locals was evident. Many, from outlying cities, drove into the little town, just as on September 8, 1844, to witness the wreckage of what once was a prospering tourist town.

When it came to damages to his own house, God didn't show favoritism. Both the churches, located on Highway 98, which was where the most severe harm occurred, lay ruined.

The harm to the First Baptist Church of Port St. Joe broke many hearts when weary homeowners returned to find that God didn't spare his own houses from damage. Some of these places of worship fared better than others. Those buildings located more inland, away from the mighty waters of the Bay of St. Joseph, came through the storm practically unscathed, which wasn't the case for the Baptist church.

Founded in 1923, this old red brick building, with the tall white steeple, had witnessed many changes within the small city, but that building would no longer continue as before Michael. The tower was bent and eventually removed and it lay on the sidewalk for months.

TABLE 36

The roof had been peeled back from the structure. When weary Port St. Joe residents returned from evacuation sites, at first they thought the landmark was spared. That was another cruel reminder of Michael's tormenting. Just the same, after the devastation in November of 2018, only weeks after taking a hit, the church did what it always does: it ministered to all the residents of Gulf County and anyone else who needed it. Hungry homeowners stopped for a free lunch there. This house of worship was one of many locations that supplied food to the famished.

In 1923, only twelve people gathered to worship at this lovely Baptist church, which had just been founded on a site that stood near the bay. Today, it welcomed over seven hundred members. Both the sanctuary and educational space were constructed in 1959. During the week, the church served as a school auditorium, but on Sundays, worshipping the Lord took center stage.

After the departure of Michael, calls for help went out quickly. Many members rushed to clean the beloved place where they were married or had their children baptized. All the damages appeared depressing and severe, but life went on. So did the church. As the white steeple lay across the sidewalk, tears gently flowed down the cheeks of those who loved this place.

It's difficult to watch historic places of worship fight to survive. Those in the community, who loved God, whispered with broken hearts, "Why your house God? You could have spared this one." Then, members recalled the words, "God's ways are not those of man." Silently, residents gazed from the old steeple to the heavens upon realizing that *God knows what he's doing. Just have faith and do the best you can each day.* Charles Stanley, the pastor at the First Baptist Church in Atlanta, often says, "Trust God and leave the consequences to him." What great advice!

The other heartbreak happened when folks drove past the First United Methodist Church located on Highway 98 very close to the waters of the bay. Many people attended the church on that first Sunday after the hurricane, knowing full well that the sanctuary was destroyed. The old stained-glass windows, lower down, were broken. The interior of the main room was destroyed. The members saw with gratitude that the steeple on this church still proudly stood over the main sanctuary, which was constructed in 1950.

This Methodist church originally founded in 1912 as a Sunday school class where members met in a two-room schoolhouse. Soon, meetings switched to the historic Port Inn until a wooden church was constructed on the corner of Seventh Avenue. This beloved landmark called to those who passed, "This is Port St. Joe. Welcome!" Gulf County took such pride in the American colonial design showcasing Greek Revival columns and cornices that faced cool blue waters. In this place, not only was the spirit was soothed but so was stress and apprehension.

In 1938, the Reverend Peter William Gautier, the minister of First Methodist, served as chaplain at the state of Florida's first Constitution Convention. History abounded in the old town by the Bay of St. Joseph. The new church stood proudly after its completion in 1950. It represented the best of Port St. Joe, although the earlier town itself was wiped from the map in 1844. However, keeping this town down proved to be an impossible task.

Thank God that the current minister, Geoffrey Lentz, and several church members had a dream. Reverend Lentz hoped to build a Great Hall. This sprawling, beautiful building would blend perfectly into the original architecture. After more than two years of problems and delays, what greeted the city was unlike any other place. Thomas Jefferson would have smiled as he saw the resemblance to his beloved Monticello.

The new Great Hall, finally completed in February 2018, only eight months before disaster hit, allowed the congregation a pristine place to meet. If Pastor Lentz had not fulfilled the dream, the years after Michael would have been very different. A small group of dedicated members led by a young, bold pastor did much more than provide a place for continuous worship; they contributed to the entire

TABLE 36

area a place for meetings, weddings, yoga classes as well as all activities a thriving community needed.

Today, residents of Port St. Joe remain just as determined to rebuild their beloved town like those in the past. At present, plans aren't certain about whether to repair the old sanctuary or completely reconstruct it. One thing is for sure, life goes on, and God knows that he is loved in this small city.

As James and Claire McKay returned from evacuation, the couple stopped at this place that held their hearts before they even ventured to assess the damage at their own home on the cape. At that time, the devastation of the old Methodist church stared them in the face. The next day, Sunday, the couple again drove to the old red brick building. They were very aware of what waited and that no one else would be present, but after many years of attending church each Sunday, it felt necessary to congregate there. Surprisingly, a few other couples did walk around the church with heads down. No one spoke. There weren't words to convey feelings. Soon, all of them drove away. James and Claire remained silent. Why had they gone? God knew.

18

T he shell-shocked pregnant woman of Gulf County found it hard to believe she was forced to leave her home to seek admission at a local shelter in order to find safety from the approaching hurricane. The little house that she rented was old. She wondered if it would survive a Category 5 onslaught. Never had such an action been required of her. What other choice existed if she wanted to guarantee her child's safety? Laura cradled her baby bump. There had been some issues during her thirty-five-week pregnancy, now this. What would all this stress produce for her and the child she carried? Would she go into labor early? Only more pressure seemed to weigh upon her slim shoulders as she walked to the old door. Crowds of people swarmed around the space with the same intention. Laura sadly shook her head and rubbed her stomach.

"Oh good, another pregnant lady, leave it to us to get pregnant right before one of the worst hurricanes ever to hit our area, right?"

Laura wasn't interested in talking to the young woman who now marched by her side. The scared mother-to-be needed to find a peaceful spot to organize her thoughts, which were many. Immediately, it became apparent that no quiet existed here, not in this overcrowded place. Constant chattering surrounded the young woman.

Laura noticed cots filled the room, but there didn't seem to be an empty one. *This can't be happening. Surely, at least, I'll be able to locate an*

TABLE 36

empty cot. I so need to lie down. Her eyes scanned the room again, but there weren't any available cots.

I knew I should have arrived earlier. If only I hadn't waited to prepare my house for the hit until the last minute. What will I do?

Frantically, the young woman searched for a supervisor. *How do you spot who's in control?*

"Excuse me, do you know who's in charge?" The man whom she questioned pointed to another woman who appeared dazed. *Her answer won't be good.*

"Excuse me, I'm searching for an empty cot. Can you help me?"

"What? I'm sorry, I'm doing about five things at the same time. A cot? No, there aren't anymore. You should have arrived sooner." The older woman turned and walked away.

"Wait a minute, please. I'm thirty-five-weeks pregnant. Surely, you can find a spot for me?"

"Do you see the number of people here? There are *no more* cots and won't be anymore, not now. It's too late. Who could have prepared for this many?" Again, the frustrated woman turned on her right foot as she hurried away.

Laura also turned. Her eyes spied many elderly people propped against the walls. The faces of these tired men and women appeared shocked, which was the way Laura felt. The woman, whom she'd met earlier, the other pregnant lady, approached. "They told me that I couldn't have a place to lie down. What are we supposed to do? Can't they find an empty one for the pregnant women?"

"I know it's horrible. Can't this place help these older people?" Laura pointed toward the wall, which supported tired faces. "The floor in this gym is so hard, and the elderly are forced to seek rest here? We're going to have a rough few days. Just pray that Michael will be fast." The two women saw an empty place by the wall and rushed to claim it. At least, they could find support for their tired backs. As they sat together, time seemed to stand still. The room was hot and began to smell with perspiration. Laura rubbed her head with her right hand while gently rubbing her baby bump with her left one.

Those circular motions provided a little comfort. This same action was the way she relaxed at home.

Once the storm hit, it sounded as if there was a train outside as fierce winds beat the school. Torrential rains fell. Some of the chatter inside the structure stopped as the nonsensical talk changed to quiet prayers. Slowly, petitions and pleas filled the space. Laura thought that things couldn't get any worse.

"Okay, everyone, listen up, the water has been turned off. If you need to use the restroom, you'll need to go outside. The commodes are overflowing." It was early in Michael's landfall in Port St. Joe. *How much worse can it get?*

Laura rushed to the toilet, hoping to use it quickly but what greeted her caused severe retching. The commodes overran with urine and feces. It was not a pleasant sight as the smell took her breath away.

"What? Did I understand that we can't use the bathrooms? What are we supposed to do? Surely, they're wrong about this." Her new friend, Jenny, appeared scared.

"No, they aren't wrong. Just go in there. You won't stay long. I guess no one could equip for this many people. There's nothing for us to do but go outdoors or wait until the generator starts."

"What's the speed of the winds? We could die if we go out there?" a man yelled angrily in disbelief.

The supervisor lowered her head and rushed away again. Silence pervaded the once lively scene. Heads bowed as people stared at each other in sorrow. *This can't be happening. All this feels inhumane.*

"Whatever you do, don't go outside! The wind will pick you up and blow you away. There are still folks going out behind cars by the bleachers to relieve themselves. This place is hell!" A woman entered with her hair standing on end. She, like all the others, appeared at her wit's end.

Laura abandoned all modesty as she held herself so that she wouldn't need to go outside, but how long would that work? Hours dragged on as the assault outside continued. The locals looked at each other, wondering how much more they would be forced to endure.

TABLE 36

"Okay, we've removed the Out of Order signs on the restrooms. You can use them now." The announcement that evening was a relief as the sound of a generator greeted everyone. Applause filled the room. At least, it was something, however small, to encourage them. As the day turned to early evening, many stomachs rumbled with hunger. Some people had brought food, but others didn't have time to prepare. Laura wondered what she would do now? Her baby needed nourishment. The pleasant aroma of food wafted through the air. Laura rushed to get in line. As she approached, she heard the harsh words, "There isn't anymore. Go back to your places."

After hours of such chaos, the young expectant mother was no longer surprised by the lack of supplies. There didn't appear to be much compassion either. Hanging her head, she trekked back to her spot by the wall. Her new friend hadn't received food either. Side by side, they stretched out on the hard floor hoping tomorrow would be better.

At another shelter, Doris remarked that no Red Cross workers were to be found. She related a similar incident at the restroom where she sought relief. She said that residents trudged outside while trees and light poles fell to the ground. At one point, at her shelter, a piece of the roof broke off and flew toward her, and heavy objects slammed into the doors that protected the shelter. The Out of Order signs there were also removed an hour after the onslaught.

No one was playing the blame game. The experiences above happened in the early stages during and immediately after the brutal landfall. *How long would the water be turned off? How many more victims would come for assistance? Without adequate water, how could the commodes be flushed?* It took a while for plans to be implemented—still, the confusion and uncertainty of this degree of trauma rings through the above voices.

Preparing for this level of havoc was impossible. When help began to arrive, it soothed like manna from God to the Israelites. The joy when, at last, kind arms that cared attempted to dissipate the suffering could never be adequately expressed. The first to respond and the last to leave were Samaritan's Purse, while Cheyney Brother's Foods arrived with a semitruck to provide nourishment. Immediately, they set up in the staging area at the local high-school field as early as Friday after the Wednesday of impact. Such incredible quickness to provide aid seemed amazing to everyone.

When large military helicopters landed on the school fields the gravity of the situation drastically set in for all. *We aren't watching this; it is really happening. I'm a part of this nightmare. No, this* apocalypse *isn't a movie. The sight of so many strangers flooding our town to assist us is overwhelming. Surely, I don't need their help, I'm self-sufficient, or am I?* Not only lives changed, but so did identities. *I never thought that I would be a victim; this can't be happening!*

19

The Anglican Church, St. Peter's ACC, led by Father Lou Little happily opened doors to anyone seeking refuge as the storm approached. The welcome received there was different than at most other shelters in town. Here, dogs and cats were allowed so that families felt unified. Such an arrangement removed the worry about the furry members of families and saved many pet's lives.

The groundbreaking ceremony for this Anglican Church was held on August 19, 2013, at Garrison Avenue in Port St. Joe. The permanent structure included a forty-nine-hundred-square-foot facility comprising a sanctuary, office, and fellowship hall. The church initially met for services at the United Pentecostal Church on Sixth Street. At that time, the church functioned on a little over nine-acre tract of land purchased from Long Avenue Baptist church back in 2009. Before that, members met at the Stiles Brown Senior Citizen Center Building. Even back then, Father Little was their leader.

Ironically, after the groundbreaking ceremony, the new church's members hurried to the Sunset Coastal Grill at 11:15 a.m. There, they shared a meal with the dreams of a new church to house them at last. It took about eight months to complete construction.

On the day before the storm, October 9, 2018, Tuesday afternoon, several members contacted Pastor Little inquiring about possible shelter as Michael continued to bear down on them. Earlier, residents believed they would be fine in their homes, but now with word of the storm intensifying, they weren't so sure. Father Little asked all of them to assemble there later in the day. The small group of parishioners had been glued to the television all morning. When they met later in the afternoon, few worried much about the storm. It was predicted to arrive as a Category 2, which meant only winds of around 96 to 110 mph. Undoubtedly, the beautiful new church could easily protect them. They agreed that each person would be responsible for bringing their own food supplies, as well as that of their pets, for the expected two-night gathering.

A local widow, Lois Hanks, knew Father Little well. She had attended the church led by Father Lou for some time. He encouraged her to join the other parishioners. Later in the day before impact, Lois put her cat, Clyde, in his cage with every possible convenience he might need and hurried to the place that she loved. Already, several church members had arrived. The mood was a little tense, but with only a Category 2 hurricane expected, few were concerned at what waited. Clyde the cat looked suspiciously at all these strangers. He wanted to go home, and everyone understood his feelings. So, did they. A small Pekinese inquisitively approached his cage. Clyde lowered his head. *When will all this madness end? I merely want to go home.* Everyone inside the structure thought the same.

After everyone arrived, which was only about five or six church families, they all spread their food on a large table and gladly shared their contributions. Accustomed to frequently enjoying meals together, the small family of parishioners thought of the groundbreaking service and the wonderful meal that they had enjoyed years earlier around Table 36 in the Sunset Coastal Grill. It never occurred to them that the place where they had held that gathering would never again welcome them. Their routine felt normal and comforting as Father Little pronounced the blessing over yet another meal. No one worried about the oncoming assault because they all believed the ICF block structure, which was poured concrete, would easily stand up to Michael. As they happily bid each other "goodnight" later in

TABLE 36

the evening from cots or blow-up beds that they brought from home, sleep came relatively easy because most of them felt exhausted from preparing for the storm and collecting supplies needed for their stay. Sure, many pets cried unsure in this strange place. The cat across the room nervously eyed the big brown bear-like animal who kept licking his lips, but he was safe in his familiar cage near Lois's bed. Even those who intended to sleep on the pews found comfort because a nice pad supported them. A feeling of well-being surrounded the peaceful unit. They loved each other and felt secure living in this space. Winds blew outside, but inside gentle snores sounded in the serene Church. As the evening wore on, a few sighed frustrated at the constant tread of heavy footsteps carrying a crying pet outside for relief or the unceasing sneezing from a person with allergies. What about that one woman who cried in what she thought was a quiet manner? Shirley prayed no one would hear her. The older woman cried often. She didn't want her friends, who all appeared to be in control, to know about her fears. Night has a way of releasing the pent-up fears of the day. It seemed as if they were preparing themselves for an invader. *Bring it on Michael!* Still, all through the evening, prayers were offered for the strength of the building that held them lovingly.

Through the night, the approaching bands of the storm brought gusts of howling wind and rain. Yes, Michael was coming. Any earlier taunts of "Bring it on, Michael!" were quickly withdrawn with humility at the frightening sounds of the approaching storm.

When the church members slowly awakened the next morning, naturally all that concerned them was news of the assault that would take place later in the day. Most hurried outside to their cars to obtain the report. The weather station surprised each of them with what waited; it was totally unsuspected. The hurricane was increasing in strength and now moving much faster than the previous evening. Others in the community who weren't members became alarmed at the latest news. Quickly, they contacted Father Little. "Lou, can I bring my family to your church? The news isn't the same as yesterday.

We chose to 'ride it out' but now, I'm not so sure of our safety." As the day progressed, desperate strangers arrived as they sought protection for families and pets.

"This isn't my church. This place is God's house. You are more than welcome. Please bring all your supplies for your family and feel free also to bring pets and all they may need." There wasn't a television in the building, but it wouldn't have done any good. In the beginning, power ebbed and flowed before going out. Again, church members had planned for this by bringing lanterns and flashlights. They wouldn't be left in darkness.

Around lunchtime the next day, as the winds howled huge pine trees surrounding the gray building broke like toothpicks. The church continued to stand faithfully against the blows. Around 4:00 p.m. conditions outdoors calmed enough that several of the men decided to venture back to their homes to check on things. They sped back to the church with news that all the surrounding roads were blocked. Everyone realized at that point that they were dealing with a killer. Totally isolated from the world with no reports from the outside, the small group huddled together for support. Prayers from the good father rose around them. Father Lou prayed for their safety and that of the community. *How much worse can this become?*

Much later, safe inside the church, they found that Michael had quickly developed from a Category 2 hurricane to that of a Category 5. With no power or water, the situation deteriorated rapidly inside. Several of the men volunteered to go outside to the ditches surrounding them to get water. Trekking through the wind and rain, the men brought buckets of water to flush the toilets. At least, that wouldn't be a problem. Thanks to the ingenuity of so many, the group had plenty of water and other necessities. The number of community members who sought shelter had grown as the storm continued. Now, there were strangers mingled with those who knew each other well. Father Lou welcomed all of them and administered to their fears and concerns.

TABLE 36

Plagued by worry over family members whom they couldn't contact and the threat of damages to homes, they collectively decided to risk returning to the houses they loved on Thursday morning, October 11. It appeared that the brute had calmed down. Many discovered five feet or more of water waiting inside generational abodes. They found fish floating in yards, fences down, roofs blown away or damaged. Unexpectedly, fires were reported around the area. With no water to fight them, the firemen turned to small lakes. Anyplace that contained water was a blessed sight. The local gas company, heroically, searched neighborhoods for gas leaks as they turned off the supply all over town. No one was allowed access inside the city due to the downed lines and fires breaking out around the town.

On Cape San Blas, a few hours after the exit of this mighty hurricane, a storm surge came sweeping across the bay with a five-foot swell that finished removing anything Michael hadn't already stolen. This massive wave covered the cape. Just as quickly, it receded. There was so much destruction from Panama City to Cape San Blas.

Utility crews rushed to the scene to clear debris as those trapped from the outside gratefully watched their efforts. To all the brave linemen, firefighters, and the local gas company, thank you for your efforts. You will forever be held in most profound regard and your life-saving work will never be forgotten.

20

Everyone who survived this onslaught will forever be grateful to not only the local police but also those who swarmed into Gulf and Bay Counties offering help and encouragement from other areas. As hundreds of linemen arrived from Florida and from all over the country, residents cheered the large white trucks aiming to return the way of life plucked from them by the evil force, Michael. Those glowing trucks demonstrated the power of our country in responding to the needs of citizens. What a blessed sight!

One resident stated, "What we saw the evening of October 10 was what we only thought happened to other people or in Hollywood disaster movies." No, it was occurring in Mexico Beach and Port St. Joe. That surreal feeling would pass, but it took months. For so many, the experience changed them forever. They would never feel the same.

"Where are we supposed to go with six pets? The evacuation centers don't allow one, but we have six! Do you think there is a hotel that will allow it? What are we supposed to do?"

Frightened and fearing for the safety of her pets, the petite woman looked at her husband, Alan. She knew he had no answers to their dilemma. They had discussed it the previous night for hours. Alan hugged her gently. The couple had no children, so their pets filled that void. They loved each of the dogs and cats that comprised their family.

TABLE 36

Margie always looked to her strong husband for advice, but this time, he appeared as shocked and confused as she was.

Finally, he said softly, "Listen, Marg, as I see it, we have two options. We evacuate and leave them, or we all stay here."

Margie didn't need to think. "I'm not leaving my babies."

Alan smiled. "I knew your answer before I asked the question. Okay, we'll stay here, but you realize, we may die here. Our house is built to code but not the latest ones. Most of the homes around us are much older than ours, but this place still has a lot of years on it."

Margie smiled. "Like us?"

The couple had made their choice. There was no going back for Margie and Alan. Once Michael made landfall, venturing outside would be suicidal. While the storm progressed toward land, the conditions outside grew more dangerous. The couple realized that now there would be no options. Three of the dogs ran to them for attention while two of the cats strutted into the room. Both the cats, who stared at their owners, kept their distance but desired the comfort of being close. Murray, the other cat, hated contact. Most likely, he remained in one of the bedrooms under a bed. Each of them appeared to understand that something was very wrong.

"I can't imagine our life without these guys and Murray." At the sound of his name, the loner cat timidly gazed into the room. Did he understand what his "parents" were saying? He would be spared the fate of being left alone during this hateful time. Not all the other animals in the community were that fortunate.

"Do you think they know something's going on? Have you noticed how quiet and subdued they are? Alan, I declare, they know something is wrong. Listen to Charlie whining." Charlie was their giant Doberman.

The couple looked at each other. Then Margie and Alan knelt on the floor and prayed, "Dear God, please spare us the loss of our lives and home. Please bless all the pets. Please, dear Lord, get us through this horrible storm. We are afraid. Dear Father, we need you."

When they rose from praying, a new calm surrounded them. Together, the couple prepared dinner, although they did not feel hungry. The storm approached with only one day till landfall at Mexico Beach. They couldn't know that they were right in its path. The gusts from Michael's approaching bands shook their old house. Margie and Alan would never forget what came calling for them. It was called hell.

Dense clouds hung from the sky the next morning. Alan immediately went outside to complete storm preparations. After years of facing similar storms, he covered all the windows with their old shutters, as they had always provided adequate protection in the past. Margie attempted comforting the pets. Something was wrong with them. They appeared fearful and without appetites, so she sang a song and rubbed each with his favorite brush. Margie's hands shook as the sound of the wind intensified.

The rain continued to fall as if a colossal bucket had been tipped. As it drove sideways in torrents, the wind also increased its vicious assault. Margie thought to herself, *I can't do this*, while her shaking hands became apparent. Alan rushed inside totally drenched. His wet face appeared deathly pale. "Margie, this won't be good. I never considered in actuality the ramifications of our decision. Now, I wish we had left the pets here and saved ourselves. At least, we may have made it."

Margie felt such fear that she couldn't cry. Her reaction was more of a "flight or fight" one; they couldn't run now. She and Alan would need to use their wiles to stay alive. By 4:30 p.m., Michael's assault was terrible. The windows shook as if they would blow away at any moment. The metal roof sounded as if it was lifting. Occasionally, something heavy would bang into the side of the house.

With the closed shutters, it was difficult to see outside even though they continued to look out the window. At one point, the scared woman lay her hand against the rattling window. She could feel it bow from the pressure. Margie had never known such fear.

TABLE 36

The pets began to howl and moan. Ordinarily, Margie would have rushed to comfort them. Now, there was no comfort left in her to give. She prayed constantly. Uncertain of what action to take, Margie suggested they get inside the bathtub. "Okay, what about those guys?" Alan pointed to the pets. He was correct. They had risked their lives to be with these furry loved ones, and they couldn't shut them out now. They had to stay together.

"Look, Marg, let's huddle, together under the doorframe of the hallway. That's probably as safe as can be." Together, they scurried to the spot where Alan pointed. Hours passed as they kneeled under the stronger section. Eventually, the pets settled down and quieted. The couple constantly assured them as they prayed for safety. Had they been foolish about staying here? Would they die? It was too late to question their decisions.

They fell asleep from exhaustion. Much later in the day, Alan gently shook his wife. "Listen, Margie, does it sound like the winds are settling?" The silence inside the room only magnified the sound of the fury outside, but Alan was right on, the winds *had* reduced. The rains continued heavily. "You know, the eye has already passed us. Remember when we heard the winds change direction? This must be the end. Margie, I believe it is almost over! We made it. Dear God, we are alive, and so are the pets."

The animals knew it was almost over as well. Luther, the big black Labrador, jumped onto Alan's chest. He almost knocked his owner over. Alan always yelled at the big dog for such action, not now. Together, this family lived to tell future generations about the day a killer attacked them and how they survived its assault. Yes, a killer named Michael *did* strike Mexico Beach intending annihilation. What the couple couldn't prepare for was what waited outside. Their life and that of their neighbors had changed forever. The monster almost succeeded.

21

Unbeknownst to Margie and Alan, their neighbors, Charlie and Shelia, experienced about the same scenario. Instead of six pets, they rode out the terror with two dogs and a parrot.

"Charlie, come on, we've got to make it to the shelter. Why are you taking so long?" Slowly, her six-foot-tall husband came to her side. "What is wrong with you? We've had all the storm preparations completed for hours. I've loaded the pets inside the car. Let's go! We are running out of time. I've read that many of the deaths from a severe hurricane happen in cars because folks wait too long to evacuate or they change their minds."

"This isn't going to be good, Shelia. Can you imagine the number of people who will try to stay in that shelter? I worry about Nicki." Nicki was the green, yellow, and red parrot whose funny antics kept them laughing each day. "I hope that he is quiet and doesn't start fussing. You know how he is. I'm not very worried about our dogs." Lovingly, he studied the rescue dogs that rounded out their happy family. Bailey, a mixed-breed, and Patty, a Chihuahua, were the loves of their life. Charlie noticed how subdued the dogs seemed. *Do they know what waits for us?*

Sadly, Shelia turned to look at their house as they rushed out into the driving wind and rain. They had rented this place for the last six years. It had sheltered them when they lost their baby at only four

TABLE 36

months old. That had occurred two years ago. After that, Shelia had refused to try again to have a child. Instead, she chose the pets, which brought them joy. What the pets provided, maybe, wasn't exactly like a child's love, but it sufficed for the couple. Charlie hadn't pushed the issue. He loved their life and did anything to keep his wife safe and happy.

When Shelia tried to open the door, the strong wind made it almost impossible. Charlie ran for the car and waited for her inside it. He turned on the lights to aid her in the early afternoon darkness. Heavy storm clouds hung in the air. Sheila could barely see him through the rain, which came down in sheets. Moving against such a force seemed impossible. The storm was hours away, but the bands rapidly approached the waiting coast of Mexico Beach.

Charlie lowered the window. "Can I help you? Are you okay?" Shelia didn't have the strength to yell back. Remaining upright on her feet was battle enough for the small woman, who finally made it to the car. Using all her might, she managed to shut the door.

"I told you early this morning that we should go. Now, the shelter will be full. Most likely, we won't be able to find a cot and space for these guys." Charlie looked at her as she attempted to brush rain from her face and hair. Her foul-weather gear looked completely soaked.

Her husband hung his head. Shelia was right; she always was, it seemed. The scene unfolding before them was like a movie. Trees bent to the force of the wind as debris slammed into the ground around them. "Wasn't that the Smith's lawn chair that almost hit us? I hope they're okay. It looks like everyone has cleared out from here but us. Wow, I pray we make it there alive."

Charlie wished she would stop with the nervous chattering. It wasn't helping the situation one bit. He kept his eyes on the road and focused on avoiding the flying objects stirring around them. What should have taken ten minutes took over thirty as they penetrated the massive rain and powerful gusts of wind. There was no one on the roads, which was scary. That fact made them feel even more isolated and foolish.

When they safely arrived at the shelter, the number of cars filling the parking lot astounded them. "As usual, you were right, Shelia. I should have listened; I'm sorry. This scenario will not be good. I don't know what we'll do if they turn us away. That old rental house will never survive this."

Shelia grabbed Nicki in the giant cage as Charlie wrestled with the dogs, who resisted his efforts. They had never seen anything like this. *What happened to the long peaceful beach days?* The young man pulled the dogs on their leashes.

"Let's get them inside. I'll return in a minute to get our supplies." Shelia had prepared plenty of food for themselves and others. Everything that the pets would need for a three-day stay also accompanied them. The Taggart family was set.

As the Taggart's approached the school, now serving as a shelter for the area, a massive tree limb fell over their path. It barely missed the little dog, Patty, who could barely inch forward in the wind. Charlie scooped her into his arms, where he cradled her.

As they entered the sprawling building, the smell overpowered them. Charlie looked at Shelia. He thought about running but looked into the baby blues of the woman he adored. They had been married for six years. When they lost the baby, Josh, Shelia's strength and strong faith changed his life. He began to attend church while he avoided the bars and constant drinking. His life changed because he saw the power of conviction in his wife. Shelia may be petite, but she was mighty.

They hesitantly entered the school, where several familiar faces smiled. "Hey guys, we wondered what happened to you. Everyone else is here. There aren't any more cots. You'll have to sleep on the floor, bummer." Brandon Hollar, one of their neighbors, strolled away.

"We have to sleep on the floor? Oh no, this is worse than I imagined." Still, Shelia moved inside the large room lined with small cots. Her eyes surveyed each of the beds. Brandon was correct; they were all occupied.

"Hey, Shelia, what ya doing? You can't bring pets here. We all had to leave them at home. Hopefully, our houses will survive. Now, you'll

TABLE 36

have to take them home and come back. Unless you decide to stay in the parking lot and ride it out. I wouldn't suggest it because of all the surrounding pine trees. It's getting scary out there; what a shame."

"What? This information can't be true. How do they expect us to leave our pets?" Tears began to fall slowly. This day was the worst of her life. It seemed possible they may die trying to get the pets back home and then returning to this disgusting place. At least, there was a generator here, and they should be safe.

"Don't cry, honey. We'll be okay. You stay here, and I'll run these guys back home. Maybe, I can drive a little faster without you in the car." His broad smile looked fake.

"You can't have those pets here. Everyone else had to leave theirs. You should have checked before bringing them. I'm sorry. No pets." The large man stormed away with his head down. He appeared hostile and angry.

"Let's go, Charlie. If we die, we'll do it together. I'm not about to let you drive all the way home and back again without me. Do you hear the wind? It is much more intense now. I can hear all sorts of objects flying through the air. I don't want to stay here anyway. It stinks! I want to go home."

The little woman picked up Nicki's giant cage as she rushed to the door. The pressure from the storm seemed to make it impossible to open. Charlie smiled with relief. "It would be better dying than having to stay in this hellhole," he shouted into the wind once he pushed it open.

As they returned home, they found conditions hadn't changed *that* much. Charlie considered they must be doing the right thing. They crawled slowly in the rain and wind. Arriving home took much longer than before. When they entered their driveway, the couple gasped simultaneously.

"Where's the roof? We don't have a roof?" No more tears from the sweet Shelia. The dogs looked at the damaged house and then at their owners.

"What do we do now, Charlie?"

"We ride it out in our trusty Durango, babe. At least, we aren't surrounded by trees here, at the St. Joe beach. This blue baby has never let me down. I've experienced some close calls, but I am here telling you about them. It may be a bumpy few hours, but we're going to make it. Can you imagine what may have happened if we stayed in there?" In disbelief, he pointed at the little green house.

"Maybe, we've lost everything we own, but here we are: well, and alive with these guys. I know God is with us, Charlie. I'm no longer afraid."

Just two houses from Charlie and Shelia, Ruth and Bob's car had floated into the street, then into Charlie and Shelia's driveway while they had gone to the shelter. It floated into their garage just as a tow truck passed their house. The kind operator pulled the car onto the side of the street. After Michael passed, the neighbors contacted the towing company with their title information so that it could be moved to safety. They were told later in the day that the car was gone. It had been stolen. Two months later, Ruth and Bob received a call from Midland City, Alabama, with the news that the Mustang was located with tremendous damage outside of the town. The authorities expressed worry over the owners, who assured them that since Michael was gone, they felt fine.

22

As the storm approached, homeowners scurried to leave and find protection for their families. Mark and his wife, Jane, decided to head for the local town of Marianna. The place was located a drive of one hour and twenty-two minutes from Port St. Joe, but during the evacuation, the time more than doubled. The couple prayed as they traveled that they had made the correct choice and that they might find safety from the monster bearing down on them. They already were aware of the worsening winds and that the storm was still a day away.

"I don't know, Mark. What if the storm follows us to Marianna? Should we venture even farther toward Tallahassee or even more? What about our car? There are so many variables to consider. I'm exhausted from loading all the outdoor furniture. I hope the motel is quiet. You don't think they will have wild hurricane parties or anything like that. Do you?"

Mark's exasperated sigh filled the car. In the darkness, of an unusually black afternoon because of the storm clouds and unending rain, he studied his wife. His heart broke for her. Usually, Jane maintained calmness with a positive attitude, but he could tell that all the uncertainty and stress had worn on her. Gently, he squeezed her moist hand. Her smile soothed his heart. Mark also felt the pressure they faced. There would be deaths from this monster. He shuddered to think of their friends. *Where is everyone now?* Focusing on the road ahead, he drove carefully hoping to avoid the tree branches hurled at him.

The couple had phoned ahead for reservations over two days earlier, which allowed a little peace. When they pulled into the parking lot, they gasped. It was full. "You don't think they gave our room away, do you? What if there aren't any more spaces? Mark, I can't take the relentless rain and wind anymore. What will we do if we don't have a room? At least, we don't have children or pets to worry about." Now, she sighed instead of him.

"Jane, don't be so paranoid. They didn't give our room away. Do you want to go inside with me or let me confirm our reservation and get the key? There aren't many trees surrounding us. I think you'll be fine here." Her beloved smile again provided some comfort. They had been together for almost thirty years.

Mark ducked out of the car as he staggered against the wind. The sharp rain felt like daggers as it hit his face. *Maybe, we need to consider moving inward permanently?* He knew they would never consider such an idea in the light of day. Mark enjoyed fishing and was an accomplished angler. Jane loved her friends; she had many. Even with the threat of death, each time a major storm hit, the couple had never considered moving. They adored this place and their coastal life.

A smile spread across the face, which was soaked. The tired man tried to shake the rain from his clothes, but it was impossible. Such a small run from the car to the motel drenched him. Patiently, he stood in the long line as pleas from other customers broke his heart.

"Please, you must have *one* room left. I'll pay double. My little girl is ill, and my wife is beside herself. Can you help us? Do you have other properties?" Desperation built as the monster hammering down on them outside continued to approach. Behind him, Mark saw others turn from the line as they rushed back to their waiting cars with the bad news, "We can't stay here. There are no more spots."

TABLE 36

The day of Michael's landfall would never be forgotten. Sadly, Mark continued to wait until he finally reached the patient clerk. The words of his wife, earlier in the car, shook him a little. *What if they don't have any more rooms? Maybe, they have already given our room away. I promised the desk clerk who made our reservation that we would arrive earlier, but we decided to help old Mr. Herman load up his outdoor furniture.* Mark's hands slightly trembled.

"Do you have a reservation?" The clerk looked exhausted. There was a small smile from the young man as Mark attempted to remain focused and positive. He said his name a little too loudly. Yes, his nerves were shot.

"Ah yes, Mr. Morgan, got you right here. Did you make plans for three days? Is that right?" Mark almost kissed the ground as he nodded. He would gladly have paid for five nights just to be in a safe place.

"Okay, you're all set. Let us know if you need anything. Anything at all; we do hope you and your wife will be comfortable and safe." The man behind him nudged him gently in the back to clear the way. Others hoped to receive the same good news that their room also waited.

As Mark rushed back to the car, a van passed him throwing water into his face. *Well, if there was a dry stitch, it's gone now.* Nothing could dampen his spirits. *We have a room!*

When he opened the door to help Jane stand outside, he held onto her tightly. The wind roared, which made even merely standing difficult. His wife was petite and barely weighed over one hundred ten pounds. He feared for her safety. "Let me get you inside. I'll come back for the rest."

What waited in the back seat almost made him cry. How would he ever carry all those things? The intensity of the rain increased, so did the wind. Jane knew better than object to her husband, for she could barely stand. Before leaving home, his wife insisted they bring plenty to eat and drink as well as gallons of freshwater. Earlier, he had objected, but he now realized the wisdom she showed. There would be no restaurants. They were on their own for now.

All through the night, Jane sat up in bed. Then, she ran to the window. It was impossible to sleep. Mark tried to remain supportive and not become frustrated with her. They needed each other. Later that night, pandemonium flooded the halls. Something was very wrong. Mark told Jane to remain in the room with the door locked. He rushed into the dark hot corridor. Someone explained that a cancer patient on the next floor had started having seizures. Everyone expressed concern for the older man. No one seemed to know what action to take. All this happened as the eye of Michael passed over Marianna. Mark hurried down to the lower floor to offer assistance, but several men had already carried the unconscious patient and gently loaded him into an SUV.

When Mark returned to his room, he shared the harrowing tale with his wife. "Wow, I wish that we could have helped him." Mark only squeezed her hand again. After a short time, chaos once again filled the halls. Everyone rushed back to the lower floor. The same group that had helped the man, as before, returned to their rooms. Sadly, they explained that the highway patrol ordered them back to safety because the roads were blocked. It was impossible to reach the hospital. Again, Mark rushed toward the sick man's room to assist as needed. The patient was a large man, who required much help. As Mark reached the stairs, the periphery of the storm passed over the little motel. Mark was barely able to stand. The only way he finally reached the safety of his room was by pulling himself back with the hand railings. Jane opened the door immediately.

"Are you okay? Are you injured? What's happening? Did the man die?" There would be no sleep on this night of dark skies and bad news. When the storm finally ended, all the customers rushed out for fresh air and to escape the scary atmosphere inside. Everyone ran for their cars, and once again, pandemonium ruled. No one could leave the motel. All the roads were blocked in both directions.

TABLE 36

Later, Mark learned that the cancer patient was so traumatized by the hurricane that he'd begun to have the seizures. Mark and Jane never learned the fate of the sick man, but they would always remember that night and the shell-shocked faces who roamed the dark hotel halls.

Black became white in all this devastation. *How many people died from the storm?* Even that is not possible to deduce. "The death toll is difficult to ascertain. It depends on determining whether people passed during the storm, or *because* of the storm? For example, Brad Price, the late county fire coordinator, is counted as a fatality *from* the storm although he passed after being hit by a tree while cleaning up in his yard *after* Michael." Tim Croft, the editor of the *Star*, showed how complicated everything became. Just arriving at the number of deaths that resulted directly from the storm, became impossible. "The best we could derive was one person in Gulf County and nine in Mexico Beach perished. There are higher estimates of around a total of thirteen to seventeen deaths." Most importantly, people succumbed to the worse storm that ever hit the Panhandle of Florida.

Yes, everything was surreal, as for many months after these events, everyone tried to function; they had to—life's demands, as listed earlier, still occurred. Life needed tending, children needed comfort, couples needed to show support. Divorces went on hold as the requirements upon everyone in these affected cities were overwhelming.

23

Vicki Higgins loved her life. Even after the death of her beloved father, Gene, she found joy each day. A student at Port St. Joe High School, the young girl had many friends and a host of interests that kept her focused and connected. The local Methodist church taught her to love God and put him first, always. With this upbringing, Vicki loved all those around her as she displayed respect and acceptance to all.

As outstanding as her father always seemed to Vicki, her mother, Rhonda, was an even stronger influence. Having come from a poor family, Rhonda appreciated the wealth and influence she received simply by marrying the "right" man. Never did she take for granted the blessings that now so easily seemed bestowed upon her. It was important to this mother that her only child understand how blessed they were.

As Michael roared toward them, Rhonda made a decision. "Vicki, we are moving to the local shelter to ride out the storm." Her uncertainty created doubts in the young girl.

"Why? We live in a poured concrete home with shutters. It is located far enough from the coast that we should be fine. Mom, I don't understand why you would inflict the woes of so many upon us. Why are you doing this?"

TABLE 36

Rhonda motioned for her daughter to join her on the French sofa facing the gulf. "Vicki, I've explained many times, and you know this. You have seen the little house my parents occupy. That is a mansion compared to where they once lived. Their good fortune, as well as my own, comes from God, of course, but he gave me your dear father. Gene was the most gracious and kindest man I have ever met, and that says a great deal. Look where we live and the wonderful people who surround us. The wealth we possess must never be taken for granted. God expects us to give back to those less fortunate. Since I heard of the arrival of Michael, this idea came to me. Let's you and I move to the shelter. We won't take space. Together, side by side, we'll rest on the floor. You and I will cook for all those people who are stressed to the limit at this time. Together, we'll make a difference. As soon as there's a break in the weather, we'll hurry home. At least, we can be fairly certain that we have a home. Think about how it would feel to question your very existence. How do you think it feels to wonder if you have anything remaining? Are you with me? I know that I'm asking the unthinkable. There are those who would call my scheme crazy, but I firmly believe this is what we should do. However, if you are opposed to it, I'll forget it, and we'll ride it out right here."

Vicki loved her mom more than anyone in this world. Usually, Rhonda was reasonable and sound in her approach to life. They felt the same about most issues, so there wasn't much strife between the two, but this looked insane. "Can I think about it? I mean, you're asking me to be miserable for several days. I already understand about kindness and placing other's needs before my own. I think I do that each day. Still, look around us. Why should we leave the safety and convenience of *this* to prove that we are kind?"

"Because without the kindness of your father, we wouldn't wake up to *this* each day. Our lives may be so different. I'll do whatever you want, but this isn't an attempt to prove anything. We're not asking for glory or recognition; we're merely showing the love of God."

When she explained it like that, the young girl understood the importance of this act for her mother. Rhonda had received a diagnosis of Stage 4 breast cancer just after the death of her husband six months ago. When she received the diagnosis, the mother and daughter decided to live their lives to the fullest. They would enjoy every aspect of being together. Vicki understood the importance of this request.

"Okay, Mom, I'm with you. What do we need to pack in order to help as many as possible?" Her bright smile touched Rhonda's heart. Out of all the wonderful gifts from God, Gene and Vicki were the most glorious treasures.

"It's funny that you ask. I have a list. Come on, let's begin collecting everything. My list is extensive." Together, Mom and daughter strolled away. Each carried the list. Hours later, they stood in the marble foyer, studying the articles they had gathered.

"Wow! Can we even carry all this inside the shelter? Listen to the wind. It may blow everything from our grasp. It may even blow us away. Mom, I'm a little scared about this. I would much rather hide under the covers and ride this thing out here."

As Rhonda surveyed the past two hours of work, she also began to have doubts. Together, the women prayed for guidance. Rhonda remained certain they were doing the right thing, so she rushed outside to move the SUV as close as possible to the front door. Immediately, Vicki ran into the storm with her arms filled with supplies. Over and over, the two women repeated this until everything was safely stored inside its air-conditioned comfort. The school was only a five minute drive. They didn't experience any problems with that except the five-minute drive took almost thirty because of road conditions and the unyielding rain. When they finally arrived, the number of cars astounded them. "Now, you know the shelter can't care for all these people. No one suspected such an intense storm." Again, Vicki filled her arms and ran into the shelter. As she entered, a burly man approached.

"Do you need any help, little lady? Are you planning on using all these paper towels and toilet paper? You must have digestive

TABLE 36

problems. That's a lot of toilet paper." Such a simple, normal joke seemed preposterous in this stressful environment.

"You're insane! Hi, I'm Vicki Higgins."

"Clyde Barlow, Vicki. Nice to meet you. Can I help you find a place for all this?"

Vicki happily explained that what she carried was for everyone. "My mother is also carrying armloads of much-needed things for us all to be comfortable." The pretty girl's radiant smile touched the heart of the construction worker, who rushed out the door to assist Mrs. Higgins.

Soon, the two entered with loads of essentials. As the others understood what was happening, they, too, hurried to help. One after the other, they rushed outside into the storm as they soon returned with more necessities. While these actions continued, the laughter began to spread. As everyone worked for a common goal, they forgot themselves and their fears. The large group unified to make this night as bearable as possible. With so much help, what was earlier a daunting task became lighter.

"Look, Vicki, you and Rhonda take a break. We can't believe that you packed all this. Let us unload the car for you." Clyde's suggestion was a Godsend as mother and daughter collapsed to the floor.

"Here, you take my cot. I've barely used it. Well, I've been reading here, but I only rested on the top sheet. I want you to be comfortable. There aren't any extras. It was early when I arrived so that I could claim one, but I'm giving it to you." Clyde's kindness touched Vicki.

"Well, we arrived late so that we wouldn't have one. We want you to enjoy a respite from the storm. I'm younger than you. This floor won't hurt me." Vicki thought of her mother. Rhonda tired easily since her cancer diagnosis. The young girl couldn't help but worry over her. "Maybe, you'll give it to my mom? She's not well, you see."

Clyde nodded. "Yeah, I thought she looked a little pale. Not a problem for me at all. If you and your mom need anything, you just find me. I'll be floating around." He smiled as he began to walk away.

"Wait a minute, Mr. Barlow. Where are you going? Why are you vacating your cot? They are precious, you know?"

"Yes, Mrs. Higgins, but I want you to have this one. I'm accustomed to sleeping on the floor."

Clyde's explanation made no sense. Rhonda understood what had just occurred. "Did my daughter ask you for this cot for me? Vicki, we made a pact. We wouldn't take anyone's space. Now, I'm not taking this, Clyde. Vicki and I are about to begin cooking dinner. If you can call pancakes dinner. Anyway, we have a lovely home waiting for us. We realize that for many of you, uncertainty waits. It is our hope to give you some peace. If I take your cot, I'm not fulfilling my mission, am I?"

Rhonda carried a single bag to the wall, which was almost filled with people resting there for support. Vicki scurried to her side. "Please, Mom, Clyde is right. You look pale. I'm worried about you."

"Look here, young lady, there's nothing to worry you. Let's get to cooking." When Rhonda stood, she staggered. Vicki convinced her mom to rest awhile and let her do the first batch of pancakes. They had eaten before leaving home, so the two weren't hungry.

As Vicki prepared a hot meal for the others, many of them ambled over. While Michael hit their town with tremendous force, the occupiers of the shelter began to laugh a little. Smiles replaced the worry lines of earlier.

The more the young girl cooked, the happier she became. Everyone thanked her for her service. Soon, Vicki tired a little. She walked to her mother's place by the wall to find Rhonda sound asleep on the floor.

"Thank you, God."

The teenager ran back to her spot. She feared someone might try to take over her station. "I'm loving doing this. Never would I have considered that such a simple action could bring me such joy."

Over an hour later, ingredients for the meal were running out as more people flocked into space. Vicki had desired to present everyone with a hot meal, but this might not happen if they continued to

TABLE 36

arrive. Sadly, she flipped one of the last pancakes. *I don't care if I ever see another one of these.*

At one point, while the tiny girl prepared food not only for residents holed up inside the shelter but with the help of a friend, she delivered food to people who remained outside in their cars due to pets or other reasons. A piece of the ceiling crashed upon her. The number of smokers who constantly rushed outdoors may have caused this. Vicki brushed the debris from her hair and continued to cook.

Tired, she persevered in her culinary endeavor. Soon, Vicki noticed that a small family filled the space behind her cooking station. They appeared to be a mother, grandmother, and three young children. Without thinking, she approached them. All of them were drenched. She carried a wad of paper towels to them as well as the food.

"Here you go. I've made pancakes for everyone. I thought that you and the children might need these." As she smiled brightly, she looked into darkness in the woman's eyes.

"Look, here, we don't need some rich, white girl cooking for us. My kids don't want your food." The large woman glared at her and walked away. Vicki stood holding two plates filled with hot food. The children reached toward her but quickly removed their hands. The grandmother managed a small smile.

"That's sure kind of you. You'll have to forgive my daughter, I hope. She doesn't mean to be unkind. I would love for my grandchildren to have this food. Joyce will be gone for a long time. She's probably cowering outside, by the covered entrance, enjoying a smoke. Your offer for the kids still available? They're hungry. It's going to be a long night."

Rushing back to her station, she found that the other plate of pancakes had disappeared. There was just enough batter to make two small final pancakes which she sprinted back to the older woman.

"Here, these are for you. I hope that you enjoy them. I've prepared over three hundred of these, but I'm so happy to feed you and your grandchildren."

As Vicki cleaned her station, she considered what happened. Inside this shelter, there was no gender, no race, and no room for hatred. "God, I'll try harder to love everyone that you place in my path. Even if they are filled with hate and anger, I'm gonna give them a break. Just look at all the friends and the good people around me. Lord, I'll look to those I love when I need encouragement and to the others when I need humility."

24

Claire and James realized something was wrong with them. They moved so slowly. Was it the heat? Everything appeared fine with their health but mentally, all wasn't right.

This couple evacuated from Cape San Blas on Sunday, October 7, with their cat, Jackson Brownie Chase. "We may as well leave like instructed although I don't believe this Category Two storm will result in much." His wife agreed, so they packed a few things for themselves and a large number of supplies for Jackson Brownie.

When they evacuated, they planned to stop in Tallahassee. As they checked on weather conditions, it became apparent that they may not be far enough away from Michael's path. Laughing and singing with the radio, the two had no idea what was happening in the waters surrounding their home.

Finally, arriving in Jacksonville, Florida, they found a gorgeous hotel that allowed them to bring their pets. Most hotels, during a forced evacuation, comply with allowing furry family members. All was well in the world of the Chase family. Even Jackson Brownie Chase appeared relaxed in this new environment. By Wednesday, October 10, when Michael slammed their beloved home, the mood in the usually sunny room was no longer light or fun. That afternoon, around 2:00 p.m., the couple watched in terror as their city was featured on television. Mexico Beach suffered a direct hit! The horror felt surreal as they prayed that lives in their community might be spared and the damages not as severe as now predicted. What they witnessed drowned any hope of those requests.

As commentators found it difficult standing in such powerful winds, Claire smiled at her husband. "You know how it is. They always make it look worse than in actuality. Most likely, they have large fans blowing on them for effect. You know?" James's usual raucous laughter didn't greet her statement. Her mate appeared somber and scared. His pallor made it sink into her mind that this was real. *It is happening.*

The couple looked at each other while kneeling. "Dear God, please spare us from this pain and help our neighbors. Allow us all to be safe, and please, guide us safely home." Arriving safely while driving home was the clincher. Would gas be available? How about the roads? Would they be passable? Many questions racked their minds. They barely slept unable to pry themselves from the images dominating the airways during the long night.

Saturday morning, Claire arose sure of what needed to be done. "Let's go home. I don't care how long it takes or what may wait for us. I need to get home and see for myself."

James smiled and nodded. "My feeling exactly. I was afraid you might think me insane for suggesting such an absurd idea. You know, the air-conditioning and water are turned off, right? We'll smolder in the heat. It may prove difficult to enter the storm area, but I think I heard, at last report, that we would only need proof of residency. We both have a driver's license. Let's go."

Slowly, uncertainly, they packed their car and headed home to their beloved Port St. Joe and all those uncertainties. Silence reigned as they drove reluctantly toward, they didn't know what. On the edge of Tallahassee, they decided to get more gas, but the long waiting lines quickly sent the message: *life isn't the same. Everything will be harder now.*

Even before they traveled far, the destruction glared at them from hundreds of downed trees lining Interstate 10. Traffic seemed to

TABLE 36

move unobstructed, but all the trees that were blown over or snapped like matchsticks enforced their fears. *What awaits won't be good.*

The conditions worsened drastically, as they entered Wewahitchka. Claire and James trembled as they witnessed the long lines waiting for gas and food at the local store.

"What were we thinking? We should have stocked up before leaving Tallahassee. No telling if we'll ever be able to get gas or food here." They felt sick and angry at themselves. They couldn't have known it would be this bad? How many people have lived through a Category 5 hurricane? When they left home, the projection was a Category 2. *How could this happen?*

Suddenly, one of their problems was solved when they saw a small gas station not far from Port St. Joe. As they waited in line, Claire and James breathed a sigh of relief. "Thank you, God!" They uttered in unison.

The owner of the small station appeared relaxed and compassionate, informing them that they had to use cash. There wasn't any power yet. This new world of darkness and cash wasn't pleasant. In fact, they decided they had stepped back into a time before so many modern conveniences had arrived.

The next hurdle was gaining passage into Port St. Joe. All traffic was stopped on the bridge at White City. Authorities checked for identification to prevent looters. Claire and James felt such gratitude to the officers for being there. As she handed her husband identification, the officer smiled. *Do people still smile? Even in this horrendous heat and disaster, apparently so!*

"Welcome home, folks. You be safe."

"Claire, we're going home! To whatever waits for us. Just remember we have God beside us. Together, with him, we can face anything." His wife tried to smile again, but it felt increasingly more difficult.

The traffic light where they turned onto Highway 98 was down. The roads had been cleared enough to allow safe passage, but what they saw caused gasps of pain and tears. In disbelief, they pointed out homes of friends, which greeted them no longer. Houses were torn from their foundations. Some slumped on the site while others had been completely blown away. "Where is everyone? Has anyone died?" The situation was in a constant state of flux that news became obsolete in minutes. Then, they saw it! Their historic church, the First United Methodist Church, still stood but sadly.

James pulled into the parking lot, although they wanted to reach their home. Would they have anything left at the place they loved? As much as they desired to see their house, they stopped to show respect for the fallen red brick building. Bereft of words, the couple sat in their car, staring at what once was a vibrant structure. Large pine trees now lined the yard covering most of the grass. The beloved stained-glass windows, which carried the names of founders from so long ago, lay broken in small pieces. Glass peppered the drive. James backed away from this heartbreaking sight.

As they passed the home of one of their best friends, Claire screamed, "Their house is gone! Where did it go?" They knew the answer but were in shock from so much trauma. *Is our house also gone?* Claire noticed James's hands were trembling, so were hers.

Someone in the neighborhood had opened the privacy gate, which was good since there was no power. Anything that they didn't have to do, any decision someone else could make, they welcomed. James and his wife felt overwhelmed.

When James turned the corner, approaching their home, they both gasped simultaneously. There stood their home; it looked utterly unharmed, just as they left it. Claire bowed her head, and James wanted to kiss the ground. They must learn to adapt to this new environment, but their lives were barely changed compared to many others.

"Claire, you remember we can do anything with God and each other. Whatever waits inside. We can handle, right?" His wife excitedly nodded.

"We are home!"

25

Kathleen Berry looked sadly in her mirror. Michael was a thing of the past. Before the onset of that maniac, she had shared life with her beloved father. She hated the monster that robbed her of the man she adored. *How can this happen?* Each day, happy memories of her beloved father came to mind. She missed him so much. Yes, her house proudly withstood the massive assault of a maniac, but her frail father had not. Frequently, she said to her friends, "I'm sorry to be so serious, but I'll never be the same. A part of me died after Michael. Just as occurred after 9/11." Everyone understood. Many lives had changed, as well as attitudes and the ability to trust.

Mr. Johnson had lived with Kathleen's family for the past six years. He delighted in the shenanigans of her two boys aged nine and ten. Kenny and Barrett loved their grandfather. It was a family knit by deep love. Jack had lately suffered from depression, which caused his daughter to hover over him. The week before the storm changed everything for the family, Kathleen's dad appeared joyous. Jack had begun attending the Senior Citizens Center.

Quickly, he made a few friends who encouraged him to go on a bus ride with them to the local Walmart. The older man appeared happy again as life took on a new meaning for him. His trip was scheduled for Wednesday, October 10, which is the day the hurricane blasted the small coastal town at 2:00 p.m.

As Kathleen listened to the worsening weather forecast, the day before impact, she struggled with what to do with her elderly father. Should he need medical assistance during the storm, what would they do? The Johnsons were aware that the patriarch had a delicate heart condition but wasn't aware of other factors that would affect his health. The father loved his daughter with a fierce love as he begged her not to send him away because of the hurricane. He needed to stay close to those he loved. Lately, he appeared to have licked his nemesis, depression. "Together we can face this storm. We've taken on more than wind and rain," he had encouraged Kathleen. Almost convinced to let him stay with her, at the last moment, she changed her mind.

Her older brother, Phil, decided to ride out the storm at a friend's house in Pensacola. Against her father's wishes, his only daughter lovingly loaded Mr. Johnson into the car for an indefinite time. Her thought was that he would be safer away from the changing and worsening weather.

The next day, unknown to Kathleen, her beloved father suffered a massive stroke. For three long days, her brother tried to reach her, but it was impossible. Without power or phone service, he could not send word of his father's condition. Her father deeply suffered as he longed for the arms of his daughter to shield him as she always had. *Maybe, he didn't understand my decision to send him away?* Kathleen would forever question what he might have thought on that last day with her and her choice to move him from her care.

At last, on October 16, Duke Energy connected the power. Her brother's call brought her to her knees. "I've got to get my dad home with me. He must feel so alone and scared." How was she to arrange such a massive feat when roads were still blocked in places by huge trees and branches?

A social worker, who was a friend of the family, delighted them when she made all the arrangements for Mr. Johnson's transport

TABLE 36

back to his home and waiting family. He traveled four hours as roads were cleared around his vehicle, when her dad finally arrived, though unconscious and unable to speak, he could hear. His daughter felt certain, from the way he perked up, that he heard and understood her voice. Kathleen cried as she held him tightly to her chest. In her heart, she knew that he had held on until he reached her side. All through the night, the heartbroken daughter sat in the dining room where a hospital bed had waited to cradle the tired man. Over and over she expressed her love as she explained why he was sent away from her. "Dad, I didn't want to send you from me. Believe me, please. I thought I was doing the best thing for you."

When he arrived home on October 17, Kathleen was shocked that he appeared so peaceful and calm. It was as though he slept. When Kathleen ran to him and hugged him, he began to thrash around, as though, he knew who greeted him. For one night, Kathleen held him firmly as the family priest visited and provided solace and last rites. Around 5:30 a.m. the next day, a beloved father slipped away from the arms of the daughter he loved more than any other on earth. Even though he couldn't communicate, Kathleen remained certain that he was aware of coming home to her and that he heard her words of love and explanation. Michael changed Kathleen's life in such a sad way. Each day, she thought of the day that Michael took away the light of her life.

26

L arge RVs and campers quickly flooded the area. Some provided help. Many who lost their houses drove motorhomes to their empty or damaged homes. Grateful to have this convenience, they found their life, at least, approached normalcy quicker than the others.

Returning homeowners received instructions to bring all their own supplies and manpower since electricity had not been restored in the early days from Panama City to Tallahassee. Unfortunately, there wasn't a Walmart, Lowes, or Home Depot for over one hundred miles. Immediately after the passage of Michael, folks wanted to get to work, but without supplies or power, it seemed impossible.

"Don't come without a generator, food, supplies, and plenty of water!" Residents warned those returning, while locating gas for those generators eventually proved a sore point. Water was distributed from nearby schools and other facilities. Local swimming pools provided a way to flush commodes. Quickly, the exact amount of water needed for flushing was worked out. "My commode requires one and a half gallons to flush." Slowly, people began to joke and laugh at themselves and each other. Those same swimming pools allowed the weary a quick bath in the evening. Modesty was thrown out the window. The temperatures remained brutal as windows had to be opened at night in place of the luxury of air-conditioning. Sleepy, tired bodies prayed that

TABLE 36

neighbors would be respectful and quiet. The days were long as the weary went to bed before sunset. There was nothing else to do.

In no time, the request from survivors to returning family members switched from supplies and equipment to the sweet phrase, "Can you bring some wine? I would love it!" Ah, the human spirit.

People lined up on the Highland View Bridge, which spanned the intercoastal. Here, they were able to find the only Internet service. A temporary tower had been installed to aid them. More cars arrived upon the good news that from the top of the bridge they could obtain phone service. Everyone prayed that the bridge was strong and could hold the weight of all the cars, trucks, and motor vans. Staying connected was that important. People needed to know their loved ones had survived, not just physically but mentally.

By day four, after the hurricane departed, hope, which was once strong, began to dim a little. *Maybe, things won't be as easy as we thought earlier.* The severity of the damages and the necessary life changes finally began to sink into the overly optimistic.

Time passed as the desperation for gas increased. Both local gas stations were destroyed. Word spread that Apalachicola still had supplies. Due to no electricity, all purchases had to be made with cash only as transactions were carried out in the darkness.

Power crews continued to be welcomed with such gratitude. What a blessed sight, as those huge trucks provided everyone one of the most needed essentials, power! The National Guard arrived on day four. About that same time, word was that "the Piggly Wiggly opened!" Shoppers waited outside as employees, with headlamps, ran through the store retrieving desired items. All sales were cash only. The same scenario occurred in Wewa and other surrounding areas.

The National Guard filed into town, and with their arrival came plenty of water and MREs, which are ready-to-eat-meals. "They aren't so bad," people admitted. The US Department of Defense packed these life sustainers. "When you're hungry, they're easy to appreciate."

Prayers rose that water supply and electricity would be restored soon. No one realized how important those simple commodities were until then. Peanut butter and jelly never appeared so appealing. Life slowed; things became simple. Windows remained open as everyone prayed for relief from the intense heat. It was important not to over-load the body because the extreme temperature remained an issue for most.

Tallahassee provided the closest laundromat. Once people real-ized they had survived, even without water for baths, clean clothes soon became important. Sponge baths from the bathroom sink quickly became the norm. Tired survivors desired a change, even if it meant driving for two hours for a laundromat. Now, even though the two-hour drive became three, it was fine. At least, momentary air-conditioning permitted a semblance of normalcy during their trek to the state capital. Even while enjoying such a small convenience, that ugly imposter guilt created shame at the thought of leaving neighbors sweltering. *Should we even enjoy such a luxury? Think of Jack and Liz. We should have asked them to come with us.* Survivors were now used to being denied everyday conveniences.

By day seven, the most wonderful news circulated. *Is it true that we may have water by the end of the day? Are our prayers answered so quickly?* It appeared impossible this could be true. Crews had gotten the water pump working on the cape. Without much ado, water lines received testing with hopes that they would soon provide this desperately needed asset. Since the cape drew power from Apalachicola, they re-ceived their water before Port St. Joe residents, who had to draw water from Panama City.

By day nine, on Cape San Blas, happy residents celebrated both the arrival of power and water. *Think of it, hot water and our own power supply!* On day twelve, the north end of the cape opened, allowing those homeowners to assess their damage. "I don't even miss some of the stuff that I lost. Funny, I can live without most of it. The sparseness appeals to me." Life became more normal each day as adjustments were made for the losses. If it was false bravado, everyone understood the importance of remaining focused and positive. There was no room for complaining and weakness.

TABLE 36

About fifteen days later, large piles of trash and debris collected on narrow roads as more and more people arrived to begin the daunting task of cleanup. Many had lost brooms and mops, but they were easily shared and circulated.

The restaurants in Port St. Joe soon opened. This action really bumped the morale of everyone. Now, affected residents could work longer hours without worrying about preparing food. How wonderful to see the beloved faces of the wait staff. Just knowing these incredible friends had also returned provided such a sense of peace. Not only the restaurants but other establishments also delighted that their customers had returned. Vendors once again made money, as they were able to provide those desired items here, at home—no more long drives for the simplest of articles needed for survival. *Could life be returning to normal after only fifteen days of being hit by a Category 5 hurricane? Impossible?*

Fifteen days, after Michael blew through the Panhandle, two people returned home. They had enjoyed little sleep since that scoundrel Michael turned toward their beach home at Mexico Beach as they sat glued to the television each night at their permanent home in Knoxville, Tennessee. What unfolded before their eyes felt impossible. Days passed before they cautiously drove down roads, littered with parts of homes and other trash, and an indescribable sadness assailed the two. Quietly they drove the distance with little conversation, unlike their last two trips when such giddiness accompanied their journey.

Finally reaching their destination, this shell-shocked couple, Barbara and Jim Oates, slowly walked into the doors of a place where family dramas had unfolded for decades. This October, their family didn't accompany them. They had arrived in their motor home only a few hours earlier not for fun or for creating family memories but to clean up a special place.

Sadly, their lovely home on Mexico Beach no longer greeted them. A stranger stared sadly from a heap of wreckage. The entire front of their older beach home, facing the water, no longer existed.

When the large RV pulled into the drive, the silky blue-green waters greeted them. "How could those peaceful waters, which we love so much, destroy our community?" Tears fell from tired eyes. *Should we hate those waters that tricked us into peace and complacency?* Barbara emitted small gasps of pain and little moans. Jim often turned to see her wet face. He couldn't save her from this one. He touched her hand often while they stared at the stranger. There wasn't much comfort available from him because his heart also broke.

Jim and Barbara had inherited this big old boxy home from Jim's family upon the passing of his mother. How many summers and holidays had their family rushed to the solace of this mecca? Never had anything unhappy occurred. This place was the family's, "happy house." In fact, they had named it the *Happy House.* Today, it didn't appear so happy.

Slowly, they walked toward the sunny yellow structure. Barbara had not expected such a joyous sight when they first rolled into the driveway. All around them, other homes had been destroyed, but their place remained untouched. "How can this be?" Such happiness filled her heart. "Jim, just look at it! The *Happy House* stands. We can move back into our home. Look, the roof appears intact, I can't believe it. After a little cleanup, well, we'll be back in business." They grabbed each other and hugged tightly.

When they walked up the steps, the many wooden steps shook. "Well, this is easy to fix. The steps are a little loose, no big deal." Again, the two hugged with profound relief. Jim unlocked the door; they rushed inside. Something was very wrong. *Is this our home? It can't be ours. Everything looks so strange!*

The entire front, which faced the water, was sliced from the structure. When Jim and Barbara studied the home, from the back on the roadside, everything appeared normal, barely damaged, but that was not the case. In a split second, their world descended from joyful to catastrophic. Their home was virtually gone. Sadly, they turned to each other in disbelief. "What a cruel trick of fate to make us believe our place had ridden out the storm unscathed when all the time it

TABLE 36

was destroyed. I would have rather arrived and seen the destruction at once. That would have been easier to accept; this deceit feels unbearable. Just like those innocent waters that playfully beckon to us. How can life change in merely a second?" Again, they faced each other for comfort, but none existed.

With no further words, the couple meandered down the stairs. They didn't bother to lock the door. "If anyone wants the remaining articles, *please, take them.*" Looking at the place that provided them with such happy times now broke and saddened them. Hours passed as they sat in their RV. Gradually, the hours ticked by in their home on wheels. Once again, the human spirit pulled something magnificent from deep inside.

"Well, at least we have this trailer. Do you realize how blessed we are? What if we had arrived thinking our place was untouched expecting to move back inside it? What would we have done then? I'm thankful you listened to the news all that time when I criticized you for wasting time. Thank God you insisted on stocking up on so many essentials. We'll be very comfortable until we can rebuild. At least, this is a second home, not our only one. Think of all our friends and neighbors who lost their only place and everything they own. Surely, we can't grumble; plus, we have this beauty to live in while we supervise the builders. Yes, we'll be fine, my darling."

Barbara breathed a little easier while gazing around the shiny new RV. Hearing the encouraging words from her mate meant life was on track for them. Together, they had survived some pretty hard blows from life. This tragedy was just another one. Lovingly, they bowed in prayer as they opened the windows of their mobile home. "Thank you, dearest Father, for being with us yet again. Forgive our weakness earlier. Our fears may have shaken us, but we're okay because you filled our hearts with strength and hope as you promised to do in these times of terror." Jim helped his wife rise from the floor. No longer were they as spry as before. That's when Jim decided they should visit Pepper's. Neither of them thought the restaurant could open so quickly, but they needed a diversion. A drive, although it would force them to witness the desolation of Port St. Joe, would be difficult, but that's what they needed. If the restaurant wasn't opened and it probably wasn't, well, they must do something.

Slowly, they drove down the street until they located Reid Avenue. Their favorite restaurant had indeed opened with no signs of damage. Pepper's was the first to reopen. In great surprise and with gratitude, they entered to the sound of normalcy. People appeared unaffected by the burden of mere survival. Smiles abounded in this place of tinkling glasses and pleasant aromas. Plates gently touched the table as delicious dishes of piping hot food were served to familiar faces. "Look, there are Beth and Charles. Isn't that Becca and George? Oh, Jim, many of our neighbors have already returned. I thought that I wanted to be alone, but, maybe, we should join them?" An enormous smile spread across her face as Barbara's dear friend Macy gently took her hand.

"Yes, please, do come and join us. We need to hear all about what you've done and your return trip here. Boy, we have an adventure to share with you guys. You won't believe what happened earlier today on Interstate 10 as we left Tallahassee."

Daniel, their favorite waiter, rushed to hug Barbara. "I'm so happy that you have returned! Do you want a large iced tea? How's your home?"

"Don't ask. It's not good." Easily she brushed aside the earlier misery. Just being with friends provided solace enough to buffer worn spirits. Yes, God worked in Port St. Joe by reuniting broken souls through the gift of friendship. Many other stories waited to be told.

As various restaurants continued to open, the rumor spread that the Sunset Grill would not. After so much loss, nothing felt shocking. The news saddened everyone as they all wondered where the little fake spruce tree ended up—hopefully, unharmed and standing inside someone's home still bearing the cheesy decorations. They chuckled at the thought.

27

Curfew was quickly established from sunrise to sunset in order to prevent looting. This action was deeply appreciated by all, especially those who couldn't check on their empty homes. Law enforcement vigilantly applied their rules as officers arrived from all over the country. The fact that there was only minimum robbery during the evacuation period was not a surprise because of the heightened security.

One set of cape owners returned to find someone stole their boat. In a land where such things happened rarely, it hurt, even more, to encounter this after such a harrowing catastrophe. There were others, of course, but most people had already endured so much, what was another loss?

Supreme frustration resulted from limited cell phone connectivity. Once life began to assume an even tenor, family members had to be alerted to conditions there. Calls passed through briefly only to be lost. "Mom, you have to talk quickly! Our connection may only last a second. I'm calling to let you know that—" Locals shouted into phones. Texts from family and friends flooded their phones but the fact that they could not open them was discouraging. The world watched, unable to help with so many of these everyday problems.

Almost everyone felt amazed at how quickly recovery began. In no time, trucks rolled back to stock the empty shelves of convenience stores. Road crews resembled worker bees as they seemed to be everywhere, clearing debris and trash from the roads.

An employee at Bill Cramer Chevrolet stated that the number of flat tires skyrocketed. "One lady had to have her brand-new Cadillac towed back to us. Every tire was flat from roofing nails. That hefty warranty on those fancy new cars can't cover that problem."

All over town, people searched for air machines to pump up deflated tires. They were hard to find. All such apparatuses were torn from previous sites by the worst hurricane in Panhandle history. Since both gas stations were down, just locating air became a problem. Even when one of the locations reopened, they didn't restore the air suppliers. Instead, the focus was on rebuilding the demolished store. Triage just happened. It wasn't planned.

Even the simplest of chores became tedious and more complicated. Most citizens realized "We're in this together." The Port St. Joe Strong Facebook page helped provide answers. When every possible remedy was exhausted, the dilemma was posted online. Usually, within hours, there would be an answer.

Slowly, the downtown bakery returned. Enjoying a cup of java was vital. Those who treasured fresh goodies with their morning coffee shouted from rooftops when they came back. "We were so afraid that you may not reopen. When I saw that sign, well, you know what? I cried."

Once the road was reopened, on Cape San Blas, vendor trucks rolled carefully onto the damaged streets, but they were coming. The little doughnut trailer also opened to great applause so Port St. Joe and the cape had their sweet tooth covered. Life began to feel normal as the Trading Post and Scallop Cove, both beloved, opened their doors. How wonderful to grab a snack or lunch at either place.

One of the most joyous openings was when the Piggly Wiggly and BlueWater Outriggers unlocked their doors. The entire town suffered with the owners when residents witnessed large boats and a ton of sand filling the parking lot immediately after Michael. Quickly, the debris was removed.

TABLE 36

One of the employees, a native of Illinois, singlehandedly filled almost one hundred sandbags. He lined the back and side of the BlueWater store with them to save merchandise from damage. Everyone learned that as they prepared for a catastrophic event, something or other was sure to be forgotten. The outside of the store was ready for Michael, but several of the skylights busted from so much pressure. Nevertheless, little damage occurred inside.

Inside the Piggly Wiggly, a few of the drains filled with stormwater, which eventually drained. The floors were soaked in bleach and mopped repeatedly. Today, filled sandbags wait in storage so that in the next emergency the stores will be prepared. Michael changed many lives as local citizens thought of the future and the possibility of such catastrophic events happening again.

28

Slowly, the massive shaking calmed. Trembling hands steadied, but it took time. Each one healed in their own way at *their* speed. As in grieving, there is no right way.

Residents, who heeded the announcement to evacuate felt glad they heeded the warning. When they left their homes, they had no idea how quickly Michael would intensify. Many who left thinking a Category 2 would be about as severe as it would get were shocked. That was on October 8. Then, the beast charged the Yucatán. Who would expect that floundering storm to progress into one of the most powerful in history? Not the residents of Port St. Joe and the surrounding areas; the suddenness only added to the shock.

Warnings were issued for residents not to return too quickly. There was no way of preparing them for what waited and the number of necessary supplies that they must bring. So many problems existed for those returning. Hopefully, they brought identification, which proved they owned property in the vicinity or they wouldn't be allowed access to them.

Hastily, food was removed from thawing freezers in an attempt to save some of the perishables. There were no reports of food poisoning, and questionable frozen packages of food were gratefully digested. Upon word that Home Depot was selling supplies from the parking lot in Panama City, cars of excited people made the

TABLE 36

forty-mile drive. Although the mileage remained the same, the time to arrive had doubled. Roads flooded with a substantially larger than the usual number of motorists. Everyone just desired to get back to normal. Most of them had lost valuable tools needed for rebuilding.

Around Tallahassee, signs of the devastation became apparent. Conditions only worsened as returning travelers approached Blountstown and went deeper into Wewahitchka. Tears fell at the wicked destruction from this hateful storm. People held their stomachs and cried at beholding the debris that confronted them, and their neighbors suffering added to the misery. Entire patches of homes, in Port St. Joe and Mexico Beach, lay flattened. Once proud, Tyndall Air Force Base was brought to its knees. In Parker, Cedar Grove, and all the way to Panama City and surrounding areas, horror replaced beauty.

Residents walked the streets in shock. It became apparent that the homes that were built to code, the newer buildings, fared much better than the older ones. Cape San Blas, although damaged, demonstrated the importance of building on pilings and following the code. Most new construction on Cape San Blas suffered minimal damages. The problem, on the cape, was that it lost so much sand. The issue of beach renourishment received great attention for months, before the arrival of Michael, but constant issues prevented the much-needed action from occurring. After Michael, houses stood so high from the loss of sand it was impossible to enter them. These gorgeous homes appeared ridiculous as they protruded into the heavens.

Port St. Joe didn't tolerate the storm so well. Inside that little town, most of the homes were older and were not built to present-day requirements. Just driving along Highway 98 broke hearts as home after home, which faced the bay, stood annihilated. Trees fell over roads and destroyed the few structures that remained.

The same was also true for Mexico Beach. Since that area received a direct hit, the entire area looked like a war zone. Some of the newer homes managed to stand proudly but were surrounded by complete devastation as other structures were blown from their foundations. It became harder, with each passing day, to recall what once stood in the striped zones. It was heartbreaking.

The northern part of the cape was inaccessible on the day of the assault, October 10. When additional rains drenched the shore, more water got into damaged homes that were already missing shingles or, in some cases, no roofs at all. Homeowners, there were unable to install the blue tarps over their structures.

"We're coming back stronger than before!" On billboards and the Internet, the slogan *#Port St. Joe Strong* gave hope and encouragement as thousands joined a website that connected them. Everyone, whose home wasn't damaged severely cleared closets and drawers, taking sheets, quilts, and anything that may help their neighbors. So much misery needed attention; residents couldn't do enough to help each other. Gladly, armloads of essentials were delivered to the shelters, which offered help to the newly homeless.

29

Each family chose a new place to call their "own." The Indian Pass Raw Bar, the original one located at Indian Pass, was devastated. However, it would be rebuilt. The owners of that establishment had earlier purchased a second building, which housed a newer version of it. Inside that trendy place, where the weary flocked, a stranger sat by the window facing Reid Avenue. Without speaking to anyone, he sipped his draft beer and enjoyed the delicious oysters that are famous in the area. A striking dark-haired girl strolled inside with a wide grin. Soon, she was followed by a blonde. "There you are! I can't believe you're here. I've been worried. I called you twenty or thirty times during the storm. Of course, I understand about the lack of service in the beginning. Thank goodness they installed the temporary tower. People would have gone crazy just trying to get through. Well, tell me how's everything. Are your parents okay? Any interesting tales of survival?"

The stranger by the window had always felt intrigued by hurricanes. No one knew him in Port St. Joe, but he had a history of following these storms and collecting stories for his books. Arnold thought this transaction between two of the local survivors should prove interesting. The two women would never know who recorded their conversation. He smiled at his craftiness as he leaned toward the next table, where the two girls spoke quietly.

Mary Catherine looked suspiciously at her best friend. These two young women had become friends at the University of Florida and had remained so for over twelve years. Something seemed wrong with Riley, who always had so much energy and couldn't stop talking. To describe her as "bubbly" was an understatement. Mary Catherine gently touched the hand of her friend, who jumped at her touch.

"Riley, what's wrong with you? Are you okay?"

The lovely blonde lowered her head. "No, Mary Catherine, I've survived a Category Five hurricane named Michael. I'm definitely not okay. I hate the bastard!"

Mary Catherine was stunned. Her friend never cursed. Maybe, *she*, herself, did occasionally, but Riley? She never had. The friend looked into the deep blue eyes of Riley Jameson and waited.

"My parents and I made it through but barely. Our gorgeous beach house on Mexico Beach was destroyed. It resembles a pile of rubbish. Have you seen the destruction? Mary Catherine, I'll never be the same. I don't want you to witness what remains of our home. Just remember all the good times we shared there. They have been ripped away forever. I'll never be happy again. The bad news is my parents didn't purchase hurricane insurance; they bought the wind part but not the flood. Now, they aren't talking to each other. Mom is so angry that she threatened to leave Dad. She claims he was negligent when most of our neighbors seemed to settle their claims quickly. It's just awful. When they need each other's love and support, they fight? I can't take much more. Today, we finally moved into an RV that one of their friends loaned us. We have all the conveniences. We no longer have to swelter, but my parents hate each other. If I lose them on top of all the other losses, I can't survive."

Mary Catherine had no idea what to say or how to help. She had never lived through a storm of this magnitude either. Silently, the young woman sat by her friend. Often, Mary Catherine peered out the window, looking onto Reid Avenue.

"Anyway, I do have a fascinating story." Riley's face beamed. "Do you believe in angels? I do. A strange story was related to me yesterday

TABLE 36

by a neighbor. From what she described, I think God has sent angels among us. I'll tell you what she said. You decide. These are her words: 'It was early afternoon on November 10, 2018. I decided I needed a beach break from the feeling of walking in circles and not getting much "cleanup" done on my property in PSJ after Hurricane Michael. A month had gone by. I was lonely and helpless, missing my deceased husband, Larry. I was overwhelmed, to say the least. I know how the beach helps us all at times, so I gathered my chair and water-filled tumbler to go and give it a try. It would be a challenge to get there since my beach buggy had been carried out to the back of my property by the storm surge. I had pain throughout my body, my head hurt. My heart ached. Every joint in my body hurt. For so long, I had done nothing but work. I guess I had become obsessed. I drove to the beach access, located just before Money Bayou, and parked. Looking at the ocean and not the devastation, I immediately started to feel relief, but could I walk it? I continued to push through my negative thoughts. When I rounded the right corner onto the beach, I felt like I could enjoy this walk as I began to breathe in the positive sea air and let go of the negative thoughts that had filled my mind. As I sat in my old beach chair, while breathing deeply, I decided to call my soul sister, Priscilla. She lives in Delray Beach, Florida. That girl always makes me see things more positively. I was happy to hear her voice. It was calming and reassuring. As I'm talking to her, the cool north wind started to blow behind me. Yes, the breeze actually felt cool. I noticed a young boy, maybe nine or ten years old, dancing in a slow-motion kind of way toward me. He wore free-form loose clothes. What a cute guy he was with shaggy dark hair and reading glasses that seemed to be too big for his small face. I waved to him and smiled as I continued to talk to Priscilla. *Where did he come from? Which tattered and torn home did he once share with family members? Where are his parents?*'"

"Slowly, he walked closer while he picked up a piece of driftwood. Then, the young boy started to walk in a circle around me, not a perfect one, but a comforting one that meant the world to me! His slow movements and smile provided such peace to my tired and weary mind. I noticed that he was outlining his path around me in the sand with his piece of driftwood. I continued chatting on the phone with my friend, telling her what's happening. She's in disbelief like me! For a minute or two, I thought this was my imagination at work, because of all the stress, but it *was real*! I waved to him and held my index finger up (like hold on, wait a minute, I want to talk with you). Quickly, I finished my phone conversation, but by then he had disappeared! How did he vanish so quickly on an empty beach? Was he in the few remaining pine trees? *Where did he go?* I stood up and walked toward Money Bayou thinking I would see him somewhere, but he was, indeed, gone. I had such a great feeling of love and hope running throughout my entire body. I went back to my chair and took a photo. Then I realized his footprints remained in the sand as well as the not so perfect circle in which he had encased me."

"Yes, we all are lonely at times in our lives, but we must remember that we are never totally alone. Perhaps one day, he or his family will read this and realize the positive impact he had on me. I'm *hopeful* he will and contact me! Until that time, I choose to believe that on November 10, one month after such pain, God sent an angel to Mexico Beach."

"Can you believe this? That's what she told me. Her words allow me so much peace. I always knew that God loved us even during the storm when we almost died."

Arnold's attention now gravitated strongly to the small table and the sweet girls. Riley took a deep breath; finally, she smiled the most breathtaking smile that Arnold had ever seen. The beauty of this girl made him stop breathing for a brief moment. *Speaking of angels, is she one?* It seemed possible.

"Look, Riley, I've rented one of the little cottages at the Port Inn. I came prepared to work with cleaning supplies, groceries, and other provisions. Maybe, you'll agree to stay with me for the five days that I'll be here? There are two bedrooms. What do you say?"

TABLE 36

"Again, the magnificent smile lit the room. "Oh, yes, I would love that—what a great idea. I have one more story, which is awesome. Do you want to hear it?"

Arnold wanted to yell, "Yes, please!" He realized that Riley and Mary Catherine might not appreciate his eavesdropping. He lowered his head, waiting for the new story.

"Okay, well, this one is about Vince Bishop, our fire chief for South Gulf Fire/Rescue and one of our volunteers, Katie, who painted the temporary station doors at Fire Station 2 in honor of the three hundred and forty-three firefighters that died on 9/11. Well, those paintings boosted the morale of many on the cape and showed honor and respect for firefighters nationwide, especially during the ravages of our hurricane. Anyway, our Vince led the department and community through the third-worst hurricane in America's history. It is impressive self-sacrificing individuals like them that make me proud to live here. Mary Catherine, you should move to the area. We could accomplish much together. The brokenness that envelopes lives that once appeared vibrant and robust is heartbreaking." Riley's blue eyes stared into the brown ones of Mary Catherine."

"You know, I recently changed jobs, right? I can work from anywhere on my computer, which is one of the reasons I needed to talk to you. Whoever heard of someone leaving a thriving town to move to one suffering from a Category Five hurricane, but that's what I'm considering. Let's purchase a house together just like we planned in college. Do you remember our 'beach plans'? Let's make them happen now, Riley, right now! Surely, one of the things we all have learned from this event is that life is short. We can't put off goals and plans for the future. Those chances may never come again."

Arnold wanted to ask if he could be a neighbor. He decided that he wanted to be a part of this strange place. Many people flooded into the area desiring to join in the quest to be #*Port St. Joe Strong*. Everyone was welcomed.

30

Daily, the huge trucks rolled into town picking up tons of debris that were allowed to collect on the side of the road. It wasn't a pretty sight. The tons of garbage did little to boost morale. Yet the ability to deposit the trash easily in front of the destroyed property was a godsend. What were once valued family heirlooms or new purchases, now lay tossed on a heap of junk. Each day, family members worked to remove the waste so that repairs could begin. What relief when all the past was finally swept away. Now, the next step waited.

Rebuilding proved to be more difficult than anyone could fathom. Unless people were well connected, a long list waited for the many requests. Even more daunting were the insurance companies. Now, the bickering and anger flared. "What have I been paying for all these years if you aren't going to repair or rebuild my home? Do you realize how many thousands I have sunk into the promise of help?" Many residents faced the horrible realization that they may not be able to rebuild on the site that sheltered an old family beach home, which may have been in the family for years. Insurance adjusters, often, became a symbol of lies and broken promises. Of course, everyone realized the blame wasn't with the adjusters, but what about the "fat companies" that took their money?

TABLE 36

More than five months after the exit of Michael, over twenty-thousand families remained displaced. As public adjusters arrived on the scene, denied claims were reopened. The result of their work varied. Although many survivors glowed over the results obtained, others, once again, had their claims dismissed. Tempers reached boiling points in some cases; the excessive temperatures didn't help. Those were miserable times, which turned sunny days and long lazy beach days into faded memories.

Sandy Collins, a successful young attorney, from Atlanta, had just completed building her dream beach retreat on Cape San Blas two weeks before all hell broke loose. When she evacuated, her life was perfect. Now, what faced her was uncertainty as she drove to see how her dream come true had fared. Sandy had worked for years to save the money to build this place. Once she finally rolled onto the cape in her shiny new red Audi, her heart broke at all the loss and devastation. Sure, the attorney possessed plenty of money, but Sandy worked long hours each day, even on weekends, to provide for herself. Her comfy life wasn't easy to achieve. Such excitement had filled her heart when she completed the building with plans of doing nothing but enjoying herself whenever she "beached It." Now, as she drove from Atlanta, despite all the changes, she planned to do nothing on this visit but enjoy herself.

Blessed Days, her sprawling beach house, wasn't severely damaged. After all, it was built by code. Still, hadn't she just endured almost a year of workers constantly parading in and out of her life before finally enjoying the new place for only a few weeks? Michael approached the cape just after her arrival at the new house. Her plans had been to work from home for a month as she finally reaped the rewards from of construction. When the orders rang to evacuate, they broke her heart. Briefly, she considered not heeding the warning. Her home was situated high on concrete pilings and built of Hardee board. All the new dwellings sported heavy metal roofs, hers the best money could buy. *How much damage can a Category 2 deliver?* When her boyfriend called, he demanded that she return to the city. She had followed his instructions. Now, she gratefully smiled at the thought of the man she planned to marry.

The brunette expertly parked the shiny new car in the tight space under the house and unloaded a few boxes of cleaning supplies. *Not bad. I'm amazed that damages aren't worse than this. After all, it was a Cat Five. How many people can attest to the fact their house withstood that? A couple of hours cleaning, and I'll be back on the beach.* Sandy had no plans of cleaning the house herself but would phone her cleaning lady while she nestled in a comfy chair on the beach. Later in the day, Angie, her best friend, would also drive in from Atlanta. The two had been friends since childhood. Angie worked hard to become a doctor and loved her position at Grady Memorial. The two were inseparable during their times together.

"Teresa, what do you mean you can't come? I need you most to clean under the garage. It's a mess. Those workers whom I allowed to rent my house made a mess. I'll never rent my house again. I did them a favor, and they leave it in this condition? Some people amaze me. I insist you must come. My friend, Angie, arrives shortly. You remember her, don't you? Anyway, please come. Our toilets are dirty, ugh! This is your scheduled day to work; I'm surprised you aren't already here. Why aren't you here?"

The poor woman, Teresa, who lived in Port St. Joe, had lost everything. Forced to move back home into a trailer in Wewa with her parents, her life had descended into chaos. Her parents tried to dominate and take control of raising her two children. Teresa would do anything to escape their rants and suggestions. She thought she had freed herself of their control, at least until October 10 changed everything. Now, there was nowhere for her to go but back home to them.

When she moved her kids into a nice older rental property a few months earlier, she thought their lives were secure. Now, that home lay submerged in the gulf. Yes, Miss Collins was correct; she should be working there at *Blessed Days.* Many more critical issues clamored for her attention than pleasing some spoiled attorney from Atlanta.

TABLE 36

Teresa had no idea that Miss Sandy planned on returning. The attorney hadn't phoned earlier with instructions. Instead, Teresa spent most of the day helping an older customer whose little home on Mexico Beach had survived the storm but had sustained significant damages. After hours of sweeping and mopping, Teresa didn't think she could fit more hours into her packed schedule. Didn't Sandy understand these were different times? Everyone must bend a little and help out? Ordinarily, the housekeeper would never miss a cleaning but how quickly things changed in these extraordinary times.

"Look, Teresa, that old lady's problems are hers. You are also my cleaner, and this is *my* day. Why don't you come to work here for a few hours? I'm sure you can complete my tasks. Just come and clean the toilets, okay? Can't you finish that woman's place tomorrow? If you don't come now, right now, I'll be forced to let you go. Teresa, I don't want to do that, but this is *my* day. So, are you coming?"

Sandy held her breath as she waited. This situation appeared inexcusable to her. Where was the drive of the employee to always display exemplary performance in her work? She performed with one hundred percent in her office. *She'll show. Angie and I can lie around and soak up the sun, at last.*

"Well, I'm so sorry, Miss Sandy. I must finish Mrs. DeLaney's work. She is ninety years old and lives alone. I can't let her live in that mess anymore. What she's lived with is horrible. I'll be happy to come at the end of the week. Will, that work for you?"

What is wrong with this person? I already explained that my friend is here only for three days. I want it perfect for her arrival. "No, I can't accept that. I need you now, as we agreed earlier, Teresa."

"I'm very sorry, Miss Sandy, I can't. Hopefully, you can find someone else or maybe, since it isn't much, as you explained, you can clean it yourself. Best to you." The gentle click showing that she had disconnected shocked the attorney. In disbelief, she held the phone in front of her face.

Teresa quit? My cleaning lady has abandoned me? After all the clothes I gave her and the kindness I always demonstrated. How could she? What will

I do now? I'm sure that I'll locate someone. How hard can it be finding a new cleaning lady?

Desperately, Sandy phoned the few connections she had in the area. They weren't many. Hours passed while she frantically called friends of friends of friends without any result. "You'll never find anyone in today's conditions. What's wrong with you, Sandy? Our area just survived a Category Five hurricane, and you fire your cleaner because she didn't show up one morning. Are you crazy? You'll never find anyone. Honey, I hope you enjoy cleaning because you'll be doing it for a while." Her neighbor, Jack Spiegel, softly chuckled as he disconnected from the silly Atlanta attorney.

The young woman dropped onto the sofa facing the satiny waters. Today, the primary color was dark blue. What a gorgeous spectacle! It soothed her eyes, which she soon closed. Sandy had put in double hours at the office so that she could spend a long weekend with her friend. This beach living didn't amount to all it promised.

Gentle snores softly filled the quietness as the doorbell jarred the young woman awake. *Oh, that's Angie, I'm embarrassed to invite her inside this mess.* Often, the lawyer talked to herself. It was an occupational hazard.

"Angie, I have experienced a horrible day. My cleaner just quit because I demanded that she come today. It was her day to clean. Can you believe it? Some people are so rude. I planned for us to spend the day on the beach and then have dinner tonight at the Brick Wall. That won't happen!"

"What? You do realize that you have people dealing with complete destruction, don't you? Didn't you see all the devastating damage? What a heartbreaking scene all this presents. *Your* home looks beautiful. I don't understand you, Sandy. You phone that poor woman back and tell her you will be happy to have her whenever she has time unless you want to clean this huge place yourself."

Angie walked to her bedroom in the back. Soon, she returned wearing plastic gloves and carrying a basket filled with cleaning supplies. Her long dark tresses were pulled up with a dark blue bandana.

TABLE 36

Sandy remained glued to the sofa looking desperate. Angie gave her friend a broad smile as she pointed to the phone.

"Do it! Now, Sandra, or you'll go months without help. This isn't the time to prove a point. Instead, let's show a little compassion and help others. Your part is small. Get with it while I go under the house and clean some broken yard art and glass. You're unbelievable, you know? Your mansion isn't even damaged."

Angie walked away shaking her head. Slowly, Sandy understood what she was trying to tell her. Carefully, she dialed the number. "Teresa, I apologize. I'm so sorry to have been that demanding. Will you still come at the end of the week? I need you. Please?"

Teresa managed a small smile on the other end of the phone even though she felt exhausted. Purposefully, she made the employer wait for her answer.

"Yes, Miss Sandy, I'll be there on Thursday."

Sandy began to understand that things in Gulf County were different. She had better learn compassion, or she would be the one who suffered.

31

As time passed, some days seemed almost tolerable in those abnormal conditions. The heat lessened, which gave some relief to those who toiled outside. Now that air-conditioning and water were restored, people took a deep breath, while they vowed to never take such vital things for granted, never again!

When such severe trauma is suffered, PTSD is usually expected. Yes, lives were spared by Michael as well as homes and fortunes, but what about the damage to the psyche? Few considered this aspect of suffering.

Carolyn Campbell had moved to Port St. Joe, two years earlier. The tall lady with shiny brown hair turned heads everywhere she went. Her dark eyes shone with health and a zest for life She chose this area because of the locality. Tyndall Air Force Base sheltered her for many years. It provided employment at a job that she loved.

After the storm, Carolyn survived her losses without too much detriment to her life. She had earlier retired from the air force and now had a local job in retail. The store, which employed her, had not experienced tremendous damage. The Piggly Wiggly had opened quickly after the passing of the storm.

Carolyn remained in her home on Mexico Beach, where workers came and went as they completed all her repairs. Since she was a strong believer in carrying plenty of insurance, her claim was worked

TABLE 36

promptly, and she received what she felt was a fair settlement. Many of her neighbors shook their heads as this quiet woman easily began to put her life back together. While those around her in Mexico Beach struggled with finding a new home and, in some cases, how to pay extra rent, Carolyn cruised through problems. Her life changed little. Known for her quick thinking and wise choices, the pretty lady had a secret that she seldom shared in her quiet life.

Captain Carolyn Campbell had earlier served her country with three deployments to Afghanistan as a fighter pilot. One day, she was shot down by the Taliban. Although her platoon promptly located her, Carolyn suffered from severe wounds. When she crashed, her face received severe cuts. Her helmet was filled with blood. Dazed and alone for a few minutes, she ripped the bloody protector from her head and threw it onto the ground. Aware of the tremendous amount of blood that filled it, the pilot wandered away from the site. Something appeared very wrong with the captain. When her fellow soldiers first arrived, there was no sign of her.

"The captain has to be dead! Look at the condition of her plane. No one can survive this massive destruction. The amount of blood in her helmet is unbelievable." One of her friends stood holding the bloody article, as he attempted not to break down with emotion. The rescue group's realization that this serviceman, their dear friend, must be dead filled them with deep remorse. Now, they would try to locate the body.

Carolyn was confused, suffering tremendous pain from her wounds. She sat on the ground, behind large bushes, listening to the voices talking about her. Suddenly, she stood.

Her face was ripped open in several areas. The blood continued to pour from the gaping wounds while her swollen eyes could barely see. As the soldiers ran toward her, one of them, for some reason, repeated the phrase. "She has to be dead."

His words greatly shocked Captain Carolyn Campbell. In her mind, she thought, *I must be dead.* Wandering away from her fellow officers, she mumbled, "I am dead? So this is being dead? There's nothing to it."

The rescue party looked at each other with confusion. "She's alive but thinks that she is dead. Her head injuries must have damaged her ability to think." They rushed her to safety. After she was flown back to a naval hospital in the states, many weeks passed until she fully recovered. Although her injuries were severe, time healed all physical wounds, but she remained a little dazed and confused. Her doctors then explained to her that she was suffering from PTSD. This brave officer merely laughed. "I don't have such a condition. Please don't worry about me. I'm too tough to suffer from PTS. That won't happen, not to me. Just care for my fellow soldiers. Heal them as thoroughly as you have me."

Still, the memories of landing in a forest and the broken, fallen trees that surrounded her as she crashed now filled her nights reminding her of how close she had been to death. There were no other signs of mental disturbance in her life. Only bad dreams plagued her now and then.

One morning after Michael's departure, the young woman drove to her job at the grocery store. It wasn't a particularly demanding position. She only worked three days each week. Her retirement, from the military service, had left her with plenty of funds. She chose to live a simple, quiet life, free to move at any time should she choose. As she drove into the parking lot of the store in her shiny blue Mustang convertible, Carolyn noticed all the damaged trees. There were many around the lot just as at the crash site earlier in a different life. Maybe, she failed to see them before. Perhaps, something made the scene appear differently, but their sight on *this* day triggered something in her psyche. Confused, she staggered into the store. "Where am I? What's happening? Am I dead?"

At first, other employees thought she was joking. As her strange behavior continued, they became concerned and located her boss, Al, who approached her cautiously. "Carolyn, what's wrong with you? Don't you know where you are?"

"Who are you? Who am I? I don't know my name. Can you help me?"

TABLE 36

Al phoned an ambulance. The captain was hospitalized. She was immediately diagnosed as having a stroke. After only two hours, her mind completely cleared. Her memory returned without any problems. Later that night, she demanded to be discharged. The next morning, as she still had no issues, the hospital agreed to let her go home. The neurosurgeon who treated her explained that most likely, the trauma of that event years earlier, her crash in Afghanistan, did produce PTSD. When she witnessed a similar scene with trees downed as in the earlier accident, her mind had connected the two. These symptoms never happened to her again.

A strange story, indeed, but an example of the many unanticipated problems severe trauma like that produced by Michael inflicted on those who lived through its wrath. Each day, many questions must be solved. Life continued to present challenging new obstacles and struggles that constantly needed to be addressed. *Do enough hours even exist in a day to accomplish everything?* Residents of Gulf County and Bay asked themselves.

32

Eight months after the storm, a local couple strolled into Sister's Restaurant for lunch. The daily diners greeted them with smiles. Instantly, Norma rushed to set the sweetened iced tea with lemon slices before them. "Hey guys, you well?"

"Yes, we're great. Every day, things improve around here. It's starting to look like our town again." Norma nodded in agreement.

Michelle soon showed up with her usual smile. "Meatloaf, Monday, you know? You want your usual?" Again, Houston and his wife, Connie, nodded.

Sister's Restaurant stood as a landmark. The damages they suffered from Michael were heavy as were those to the homes of the mother, Sherill, and daughter, Julie, who owned the restaurant. Just the same, they were, at last, back serving hot delicious meals to neighbors and friends.

Julie walked over to the small four-seater table. "It's sure good to see you back. I heard your home sustained little damage. Wow, you're blessed. We were hit hard both here and at home, but you know that. Well, good to see you back here at *our* home, take care."

Connie bent closer to her husband. "I love this place. Sister's is one of my favorite restaurants. They suffered more damage than most. It seemed to take them longer to reopen. Out of all this destruction, I am crushed by the loss of Candace's home. She and Stewart have

TABLE 36

endured more than anyone I know." Sadly, she took a small sip of tea and gazed around the room.

"You know it broke my heart, as well. Do you remember when we first arrived here, over thirteen years ago; they'd just sold that gorgeous beach house at the end of Cape San Blas? That was one of the largest in the area, but the beach encroached so far onto their property. It was becoming dangerous for them. After the one next door fell into the ocean, I understood their panic."

"You've got that right. I couldn't have waited. It would have been necessary for me to do something immediately. Remember, that incredible red house they built? It was definitely the prettiest home on the cape, at least to me. Then, the market went south. They lost everything, like many people around the country. Isn't that when they moved to their office building in Simmons Bayou? At that time, they owned their business as loan officers. Is that right?"

Connie nibbled a bite of the meatloaf. It always tasted perfect, especially when Sherrill added extra sauce. Houston nodded as he waved to some friends.

"Yes, that's right. Candace is so talented. About the same time, due to the turn in the market, she began catering. Remember all the great meals we have enjoyed with friends at their home? What a gourmet chef she is. Surely, they will rebuild so that she can continue delighting us with her culinary talents!"

"I sure hope that she does. That's some of the best food in the area not excluding Sister's." Connie looked at her plate and nodded. "Remember when Candy remodeled their office? It became a jewel. During that time, she opened her own gourmet business with Stewart. Her husband is so supportive of her. He's always by her side. I really admire both of them. How hard do you think it was for them to close the loan company? Anyway, she has found her niche."

"You're right about that one as well." Connie nodded to more friends who strolled inside. Houston dropped a large bite of meatloaf on his white slacks. Connie groaned. "That's gonna be hard to get that ketchup out. Oh, Houston!"

"I know, I'm sorry. Anyway, shortly after Candace began the gourmet business and started to get straight, they decided to build condos in Ecuador. I knew that was a big mistake. I tried to tell Stewart, but he seemed so sure. It broke my heart what that country did to our friends. It seems someone should be held responsible for ruining their lives. As before, the two of them jumped back with excellent resiliency and faith. I remember how concerned they were for all the people who invested in their project. We've had other friends who lost money in similar construction problems in foreign countries. I guess it's not that unusual. Shoot, if we had the money, I would have invested as well. Such hard times may have torn many couples apart, but Candy and Stewart are devoted and in love. They are amazing." Houston nodded as he waved to Gidget. "How about one of those chocolate brownies? Bring me Connie's so that I can have two. She hates desserts." Connie smiled. She happened to love Julie's chocolate brownies, especially when they had an extra coat of chocolate.

"How could a country be as corrupt as Ecuador? Unbelievably, Candace's attorney over there didn't help much. Seems to me, those Ecuadorians pulled a number on them. I feel terrible not only for our friends but all the people who lost money on that investment. Those condos were beautiful, and it would have been a gorgeous place." Both husband and wife sighed in frustration.

"Well, I heard that they plan to rebuild their home here. Now, that's good news."

Gidget walked toward them with two gigantic brownies. "Do you need extra ice tea?" Her smile could melt a pile of metal. Diners, seated around them became involved in their levity. Everyone laughed as Connie grabbed the extra brownie and devoured it. Yes, hearts broke for friends and neighbors, but life began to settle for most. Even laughter filled once carefree places.

33

The house that the striking couple owned in Tallahassee soon bored them after years of jet-setting. That's when they decided to build a beach home on the bayside of the Gulf of Mexico. As soon as their house, *Shore Paws* was completed, they complimented themselves on a job well done!

Vivian Brown and her husband, Tony, completed their new home on Cape San Blas two years before Michael's assault.

"Tony, one thing's for sure, this place isn't going anywhere. A hurricane may take out the cape, but this house will stand, I'll bet ya."

Vivian Brown was more than beautiful and witty; she ranked as brilliant in her husband's eyes. He would do almost anything to keep her safe and happy. When the news arrived about the approaching gale, the couple discussed the situation over cocktails on October 8, which was two days before the impact of Michael was expected.

"Can you believe this sunset? Isn't it the prettiest one ever? I love it when the sky is colored with pinks and blues. I even see a speck of purple. Do you see it, Tony?"

"Vivian, you say that every night. Let's agree, they're all outstanding!" Her husband gently clasped her hand in his. Not only did Tony admire his wife's intelligence and kindness, but he would never forget the valor she displayed in her recent fight against breast cancer. Ever since the day they received an all-clear, he thought he saw a new light in her eyes. Tonight, the beautiful pink sunset reflected in her gray eyes.

"Now, Vivian, we must discuss this Michael character, which is bearing down on us. Where do you think we would be safer? I'll do whatever you choose. Should we remain here or return to Tallahassee?"

Not responding for a while, the love of his life dreamily gazed at the sky. "Well, it's only a Category Two, so it doesn't matter. Personally, since we've just arrived here, I prefer to remain. Don't forget this house is concrete and is on the bayside not the gulf, so I think we'll be fine. The core of landing is still unsure, so we could drive all the way back to Tally only to find it's shifted course. Let's stay here. I've never experienced a hurricane."

Even after forty years that smile continued to melt his heart. "Okay, we'll ride out our first hurricane with Mitzie and Moe." Those dogs kept them young. Vivian and Tony decided long ago that the reason they suddenly experienced a drop in their blood pressure problems, like most of their friends, happened when they got the two dogs. Mitzie ran over to Vivian requesting a walk with her particular bark that signaled a possible emergency. Yes, an emergency was coming, but it would prove to be much more than a demand for a walk from their dog. Vivian and Tony had no inkling as to the challenge that waited for them.

As Michael's bands increased in scope, the winds and rain blew with such intensity that even Tony admitted a little fear. "Wow! I've never seen anything like this. Can you imagine having to be outside in this?"

Vivian and Tony couldn't know that only a few miles away, a local family with seven kids had found solace at their church in Port St. Joe. There, they rode out the storm with their pastor's family, including three more children. Not far away from them, a husband and wife risked their lives to remain with two dogs, three cats, and their beloved cockatoo. Some may call that crazy, or maybe it takes a fellow pet owner to understand the connection of love between pets and people. While Vivian and Tony enjoyed every convenience, safely

TABLE 36

tucked inside a home built like a fortress, around them folks suffered in cramped, horrible conditions.

When the power went out, Brown's generator kicked on. "What a glorious sound! That was so smart of you to have it installed as we built the house. I love that sound."

"Me too." Tony was ready for his afternoon nap. As he staggered toward the bedroom, Vivian picked up her latest book. She was an author and loved to peruse her books for errors. It made her angry that she could always find something she missed. Outside, the nasty assault of a mammoth continued. Occasionally, the lights flickered, which only made the couple appreciate their comfy oasis.

At 6:00 p.m., Tony strolled back into the room. "I feel human now. Want a cocktail?" He noticed that his wife was quiet and clutched her recent book.

"No, I'm afraid to dim my faculties, what if we should have to flee for some reason? The conditions outside are much worse, Tony. One of us should be prepared to react with a full deck." She looked at Tony for encouragement.

"Don't be silly. We're not going to need to flee. Don't we have everything we could need except a great Italian meal?" Moe barked. Maybe he liked the idea of a scrumptious Italian dinner as well.

The first half of the hurricane passed without causing any worry. By the time the winds switched to the west, the Browns knew that due to the tremendous rains, beach erosion, and tidal conditions, they would experience a storm surge but couldn't prepare for what came. As they admired this fortress, atop fifteen-foot concrete pilings that were safely situated one-third of a mile from the bay with salt marsh and pine trees surrounding it, they did feel invincible. That is until in the space of five minutes they witnessed the waters rise to twelve feet below their house.

"Tony, wasn't that your toolshed floating past? I could declare that I just saw our gigantic picnic table pass as well. I wasn't prepared for this."

"Me neither. Who could be ready for anything of this magnitude?"

"You know my brand-new kayak? Well, it swept past as well. I hate that. You know how much I loved it?"

Tony stood beside his wife staring outside in disbelief. "Did you just hear something crash into our elevator door downstairs? I have a feeling that Michael just took it out."

They waited until the storm cleared before venturing outside, which was a difficult but a smart move. What greeted them ripped the smiles from their faces. The shiny new elevator door had been smashed. Their long sturdy dock was torn apart. Only a small section of it remained. That treasured view of the salt marsh was now filled with debris. Facing them was four inches of mud and detritus from the bay. This gunk stretched all the way up their long driveway. Feeling a little discouraged, Vivian and Tony finally mucked through the mess back to the house. As soon as they entered, that "special" bark from Mitzie told them they needed once again to go outside.

"How are we going to take the dogs out? Mitzie would sink in all that slime. We've got to get them up to the road but how?"

Tony loved a challenge. He shook his head and then he scratched the right side, which signaled he'd had a brainstorm. "I've got it! We load them in the wheelbarrow. That will be their chariot."

Vivian laughed with delight. They weren't about to be foiled by a giant named Michael. "Yes, just like in the Bible. We'll be David and Michael Goliath!" They laughed.

"Now, you're talking. Our babies will ride in the splendor of a chariot. I wish Charlton Heston could see us now!" Tony rushed to remove the wheelbarrow from its place in the storage room. Thank goodness that the door remained. "Come on, Vivian! I have it ready."

With both dogs in tow, his wife ran to accompany her husband. How would the dogs react to their first view of the place after the storm? As they looked at the war zone around them, all laughter stopped. Neither spoke. There would be no more laughter for a while.

The two dogs loved the attention as they happily and quietly rode to the road. Vivian and Tony sighed as their dogs did what they loved most, put on a show. Slowly, the sadness turned to a little joy.

TABLE 36

"We're alive! Our house, even though damaged, also survived. What more can we ask?" Later, they learned that their water and sewer system were both destroyed.

After living in these conditions for two days, the authorities announced that it was safe to travel to Tallahassee. Naturally, they were concerned about their primary residence.

"Vivian, we need to head back to Tally. The other house may also be damaged. That's a long shot, but it's possible." His wife didn't want to leave but knew he was right. The next morning, early, they loaded the dogs and drove the distance that usually took two hours but now took five because of the compromised conditions of the roads as well as excess traffic.

"Hopefully, everything works there. We'll be able to flush the commodes and drink water from our own system. Think of it; tonight we'll sleep in the other bed. I'll be able to do laundry. Life is back on track."

Again, their dreams lay smashed before them when they arrived at the Tallahassee home. If they had scuttled back earlier, they might have been dead. Huge tree limbs had crashed through the roof and attic. All that now lay on their bed with the room filled with insulation from the attic. The entire scene was a little too much. Instead of an extra house providing additional security and relief, they now faced two insurance claims and all the grief that accompanied it.

Mr. Brown had developed a few connections over the years. He immediately found a workman to install a tarp over the roof for protection from the relentless rains. Their Nationwide adjuster arrived the next day and spent the entire day with them. Faster than they ever dreamed, they received a check covering all the repairs. Mrs. Brown yelled, "I love my insurance company!" Others experienced similar news, but after a year, others still wait.

34

Tales of heroism floated around the town. No one was shocked at the selfless acts that were related. These were Port St. Joe Strong people!

As the wait staff prepared for a Wednesday crowd, about eight months after Michael's departure, at the Brick Wall Sports Bar, Vince, a waiter, appeared subdued.

"Hey, what's wrong, Vince? Cat got your tongue?"

"Naw, I was thinking about how blessed we all are just to be alive and well. So many incidents are coming to light now. I feel awful eavesdropping, but it's impossible not to do it. You know? Do you know that Mrs. Ford, who is eighty years old, and lived by herself, refused to leave her home and pets? This is an amazing story of love and family devotion. When I heard it last night, something grabbed inside of me. I found it impossible to walk away. The customers must have thought me weird, but I remained frozen for a long time."

"What, you felt emotion? Really, what's the story? This must be some great tale of woe?"

"Well, you know who she is, right? Her son is a deputy sheriff. Still, he couldn't convince her to move. She flat-out refused to desert her three dogs. Anyway, her house is located by the water, so when Michael hit, that lady gathered her dogs on the sofa. That's where

TABLE 36

they rode out the storm as waters flooded her house. I heard the sofa actually began to float. When she was able to stand, the waters were waist-deep around her. Only then did she phone her son for assistance.

"The deputy and slept at the sheriff's office because their homes were damaged so badly. During that time, they all worked every day, all day, for two to three weeks. Immediately, when the storm left, those guys began the rescue. I'll bet Deputy Ford never expected that one of the calls for help would be from his mother. He had to use a boat to rescue her and her two dogs. One of the pets panicked. As he tried to return to his cage, during the brunt of the assault, sadly, he drowned. Anyway, Mrs. Ford lost everything. Even her four-year-old car was declared totaled. At the age of eighty, she must start life again. I don't know, its stories like that which make me realize how precious each day is for all of us. I sure hug my little boy tighter each night since Michael changed everything for us."

Later in the day, a small group of women walked into the Brick Wall. Since they were regulars, they always sat in the same place at a table in the back. "I don't know about this. I'm not looking forward to talking about what happened. No offense, but this seems like a dumb idea to gather and share our Michael stories. I mean, it's been almost a year. I want to move on and enjoy my life not look back, but I love you guys so, if this helps you, I'll share my experience. You know, I'm not much for talking about myself, so I'd like to go first so that it's over. Is that okay with everyone?"

The others did understand her request. Martha White had worked all her life as an accountant. She had achieved great success. Although most people like to "toot their own horn," not Martha. The others nodded they were happy she decided to join them. "Okay, you go first. We can't wait to hear your tale, Martha."

"Okay, fine; water, wind, and fire. I swam away from our home as it literally blew behind us. That's about all I have to say. The end."

They all looked at each other. Martha was known for getting to the point, but this was exceptionally brief even for her.

Karen Barkley sighed. "Wow, Martha, that would make a great story as well as a movie. Don't you want to share the details? I mean we all want to know the story."

"Nope, that's what happened. I like it short and sweet. So, what's yours?"

Everyone sighed loudly. Martha's was probably the most dramatic tale of survival, but they all knew better than trying to force her. "Okay, well, here goes. All the doors and windows in our home, which is a little old now, are hurricane rated. Only our upstairs living door is not; unfortunately, it doesn't open out. When that brute attacked us, the door started to push open inside as the water rushed into the room. I did my best to hold it while Cassidy found some boards to shore it closed. The problem was she couldn't go outside with that massive wind. Being the genius, which she obviously is, she spied my daddy's antique bed realizing that it had slats supporting the mattress. They were taller than her, and she lugged them up the stairs as water continued pouring into the living room. Without missing a beat, petite Cassidy hammered them across the front wall and the door. Amazed at the speed with which she worked, together we moved all the furniture against the slats. It held. If that door had blown, we would have lost the roof and everything inside would have been destroyed."

Karen looked down at her shaking hands. Even now, almost a year later, reliving that experience produced heavy emotion. "Anyway, the next day, we could barely walk because of severe leg cramps, but our home by the Gulf of Mexico was saved."

Vince listened to her story. "Wow, Karen, that's pretty powerful. I don't like to relieve the storm, but every time I hear someone's story, I am mesmerized by the different scenarios. Your meal will be out shortly."

TABLE 36

"Hey, Vince, I think I'll change my order from an iced tea to a beer. One year later and my hands still shake."

"Yeah, me too, but I need to tell this. My father almost died during Michael. He only survived by standing on the toilet as the waters rose around him. The amazing thing is that he held his wheelchair-bound friend also saving him." Nancy Shook wiped a tear from her eye.

"Nancy, I'm not surprised! Your dad fought in World War ll. He is one of the most amazing men I've ever met. He's truly one of the greats."

"Yes, that's for sure. Did you hear about *my* neighbors? My husband, Frank, and I didn't suffer any damages but our neighbors, the Barstow's, what a story! Can I share that for my contribution?"

The others nodded excitedly at Joan. "Well, Mr. Barstow survived only because his wife held the mattress on which he floated aloft while his son swam to the living room to save their drowning dog. Later, I saw a helicopter land and rescue them all to safety. It was amazing. Instead of tears, I have to laugh at the incredible way people survived. I mean, after all, how do you get experience for this sort of catastrophe?"

"Only by surviving." Gail Lippard took a deep breath. "Okay, here's mine. Harvey and I are like Joan and Frank, we didn't really lose anything, but *my* neighbor, Hugh Glasson, kicked himself for leaving the family boat when they evacuated. You know how scary it was when we realized the intensity of that monster? Anyway, he grumbled the entire time they were away. When he returned, he received the most incredible news. His boat crashed into a flooded house. It saved the lives of an entire family who were trapped. They would have drowned if not for Hugh Glasson's boat."

Vince approached with their meal. "That's an incredible thing. I guess all our stories are amazing because they are stories of human resilience and the will to survive."

"Don't you forget God, Vince. Guess who prevented Hugh from remembering his boat and used it to save his friends? We should all remember that sometimes we aren't responsible for the miracles in our lives. That late start or lack of memory that we complain about may just be God."

35

fter the passage of this Category 5, so many people flooded our area. Workers from all over the country poured inside to assist those in need. What a wonderful story they all can share. Krazy Fish Grill located on Monument Avenue also welcomed plenty of diners with life-changing stories.

The shy waitress strolled toward the table of locals with her head down. The young girl was barely out of high school. Her plans for college were placed on hold. The bills that flooded her parents prevented any thoughts of her college education. The family struggled to stay afloat. As she approached, she heard this: "Yes, it was scary. When I realized what was happening, because it all occurred with such rapidity; the only thing to do was put a life jacket on my husband and me. You know our house was located on Thirty-Second street on Mexico Beach. Anyway, we swam in the storm surge with our two dogs, Curly and Moe. Talk about fear. Yes, I know that beast well."

The wind blew gently as the early October weather soothed the usual heat of summer. Finally, the weather felt glorious as friends congregated for dining alfresco at their favorite grill. Laughter and heavenly giggles vibrated from the gentle breeze as stories were shared in another location of Port St. Joe. "Well, the wife and I hunkered down in a pile of blankets inside our bedroom closet with our two small dogs. We lay on that closet floor for two hours listening to the howling wind as it tossed pieces of our lives and those of friends like a salad. Constantly, the sound of slamming and banging on the walls of our house kept us praying for safety. When the sounds finally quit, we knew from the lovely sound of peace that the worst was over."

"My story is harrowing to me. You all know that I lost, Glenn, my husband of twenty-nine years on April 20. It became impossible for me to function as I grieved for my soul mate. The kids convinced me to get away for a short time, so I went to Mexico Beach and stayed at the El Governor Inn a few days. When I returned feeling a little better, I discovered that someone robbed my place. They stole many family heirlooms and sentimental items. The items stolen included my husband's wallet. Okay, give me a moment to collect myself. I still get so angry that anyone would do this. On October 10, when it began to break, I was home alone while seven of the seventy-year-old trees were uprooted in my front yard. My plan to wait it out in the hallway with pillows and blankets around me was formed, but I couldn't move. Instead, I felt drawn to Mother's recliner. Probably, that chair symbolized comfort to me. That's where I remained as I prayed and cried, asking God to spare my life. When it finally ended, I realized that I am a survivor. Yes, I lost a lot of material things as well as my husband in that one year of 2018. A blue tarp still covers the damages to my roof, but God covered me with his love and protection. I now realize that for the rest of my life, I won't claim fear but strength."

Silence replaced the earlier laughter. "I feel obligated to share my experience, although I promised Lester before we left our home that I wouldn't. My husband is sick of giving Michael any more of our lives. He says we should 'just get on with it.' I understand his thought, but I can also identify with the need to share what happened on that day we will never forget. Just like the day of the assassination of JFK or 9/11; we'll always remember October 10, 2018. As you all know, Lester and I don't live on the beach or close to the water. Our home sits on Long Avenue inside Port St. Joe. Susie, our five-year-old, was pretty sick. She had fever, diarrhea, and vomiting. The arrival of a Cat Five was not what I needed. Worry consumed me for our child.

TABLE 36

When Dan, my father-in-law phoned to tell us that we must evacuate because the predictions were wrong. Now, they predicted a Cat Four or Five, so we loaded the car with two kids, six snakes, three dogs, two cats, and two Guinea pigs, as well as one rabbit and a hamster. All this, we packed into my dad's Tahoe. Lester stowed the other child and all our stuff into his vehicle. We all set out for Wewa around ten in the morning. My father-in-law, his wife, our friends Mark and Jaime with their four kids and dog followed. What a procession! We barely made the closing of the White City Bridge. Can you imagine if we had been a few minutes late? I shudder to think. The entire distance to Wewa, trees continued to fall onto the road, but we were able to pass safely. What were we supposed to do? We didn't have a plan because we thought Wewa would be safe. Quickly, it became apparent that we needed to press on. Later in the day, we staggered into the Muscogee Fishing Lodge. I felt like kissing the ground when I limped from that car. I once worked there so knew a few of the staff. The houses were all built between 1913 and 1925. My husband phoned me just after I arrived to ask for my help. As he attempted to assist someone else, he slipped off the road and needed Jaime and me to pull them out of a ditch. Well, we tried, but the streets around Wewa were blocked. I tried calling him, but the cell service was gone. As I worried about his safety, a tree fell onto the end of the house next door. It was pretty close. Squeezing everyone into the middle bedroom, we held our breath. The sound of the wind pulling shingles from the roof was not a pleasant one! Soon, rain poured into the little house. That howl from the wind as trees fell around us like toothpicks will forever fuel my nightmares. It was horrible!

"The moment that the wind died, I realized we made it, but what about my husband and daughter? Around seven-thirty in the evening, several men walked from the woods carrying chainsaws. I have never been so happy! Since we remained blocked in that space, I ran to the vehicle where I discovered that although sporadic, the wi-fi did work. There was no helpful news for us. My baby remained very ill. Jamie and I posted to Facebook, so friends knew where we remained stranded. One of our dear friends saw my post. She contacted her husband in the coast guard who landed and removed Jamie and her four children. I couldn't leave without knowing the fate of my husband and child. I remained with my children. After three days of not knowing what may have happened to him, the sheriff's office sent someone to clear the roads.

"At last, I was free. Obviously, there's a happy ending. I located my husband. We all survived a Cat Five but are here to tell about it. Yes, we lost everything, but we have each other. I'll never put stock in material things again. Thanks to a freak, I know what's important and thank God each day."

36

One year after Michael destroyed our way of life. A Gulf County resident, Missy Blanchard, offers her story. Here's her experience: on that fateful day of October 10, 2018, when the sun began to rise, the winds already blew with high intensity while the rain descended in blinding sheets. My oldest son, Chip, and his family spent the night with me because they lived in St. Joe Beach. The other son, my youngest, Donnie, decided he and his family would be safe if he remained at the beach house. Of course, his news upset me.

As the storm intensified, I called him, describing what I witnessed as trees blew over, and the roofs of neighbor's houses ripped away before my eyes. While I begged him to join us, one of the trees, which concerned me, a huge pecan tree in my yard began to sway. That behemoth rocked with the massive wind gusts. I explained to Donnie that the tree appeared ready to fall. Donnie begged me to seek protection from that possibility. At that moment, my old pecan tree fell only three inches from my window, causing the phones to disconnect. Over and over, I attempted to reach Donnie so that I might calm his fears. After all, the fall of the tree missed me. I remained fine. Now, I feared for my son, who refused to leave the beach.

Unable to stop crying, I found solace in my rocking chair, which is a place of comfort for me. Chip, my oldest, who stayed with my husband and me, held me as objects flew past our windows. Together, we prayed the Lord's prayer while listening to Michael's savagery increase. At this time, we couldn't see Highway 71, located directly in front of our home, due to the abundant rain which plummeted us. Reports later stated that the wind blew at 175 miles per hour with gusts at 200 mph. Our home began to lift. It reminded me of The Wizard of Oz as I attempted to save my two granddaughters who huddled on blankets and pillows in the hallway. Our location was twenty miles from the beach.

My thought was that if we suffered these terrible conditions, what happened to Donnie? The next day, October 11, was his twenty-third birthday. Around 3 pm CST, the storm calmed. It appeared to end for us. My husband and I, with our other son and family, decided to locate Donnie. We had to know if he survived. St. Joe beach roads were covered with trees and debris, which made it impassable at that time. Our only choice was to locate CR386, but we couldn't identify it due to all of the destruction. While we tried to decide a course of action, more people arrived with chainsaws and axes. Probably about fifty people worked to clear a few feet of the road. While the men cut the giant trees, the women attempted to pull them out of the path. We drove our trucks over the semicleared surfaces. For eleven hours, we worked as we tried to travel over Highway 386. Eventually, we were forced to abort our efforts when we arrived at the bridge. There, so many of the trees covered the Overstreet bridge. We feared that someone might be killed since they stacked on top of each other.

When we decided to turn around, planes flew over Mexico Beach and St. Joe Beach. I told my husband that I would find Donnie if I had to walk. Fear controlled my thoughts. Still, we turned around and drove back over all the work we earlier accomplished toward Highway 71. Severe flooding made it impossible to continue our efforts. My husband, Mick, remembered the commercial road that connects the two bridges. Other residents had cleared those roads. Slowly, we proceeded toward the beach.

TABLE 36

After hours, we arrived at Chip's house, which was completely blown away. Thank God, he stayed with us. My fears for Donnie intensified as I witnessed this destruction. Next, we located his condo. It also was utterly devastated. Now, we didn't know what to do.

All I could think of was our church at Beach Baptist Chapel. We agreed to check there. It was 3 am when we entered the darkened building. People lay in church pews trying to sleep, which looked impossible. I lost it! Screaming and crying Donnie's name, I became inconsolable. A member of the church wanted to calm me to no avail. Finally, he grabbed me with the best news of my life. "Donnie is in that room with his family." He pointed to another dark space. Suddenly, like an apparition, my beautiful son walked toward me. His face covered with tears. We couldn't speak. All we could do was tightly hold each other.

Through my emotion, I explained my fears that he may be dead. Donnie's crying became louder as he sobbed, "Mom, I thought you were dead! The last words I heard were that the tree was falling on you. Then the line disconnected." My mind couldn't comprehend the fear he felt. His wife, Katie, whispered that Donnie fell to his knees with grief when he lost my call.

That monster may have taken both of my boy's homes and everything they owned, but the clothes they wore. Still, my God kept his hands protectively surrounding us. Donnie lived to celebrate his twenty-third birthday. Yes, conditions tested us once again after the storm. Working with the insurance adjusters and cleanup brought us back to our knees, but I kept my faith while knowing that things will improve. After all, we are 850 Strong!

37

On August 24, 2019, another mammoth developed from a tropical wave. This one began in the Atlantic Ocean. It would become the first hurricane of the 2019 season. What a monstrosity it quickly became! It intensified as it moved toward the Lesser Antilles before being labeled a hurricane on August 28. Two days later, on August 31, it was called a major hurricane. On the following day, it reached Category 5 intensity as our nation trembled to watch another ogre speed toward the United States. The sustained winds were one 180 mph. On September 1, at 4:40 p.m., the assault began from Hurricane Dorian.

The first place it hit was the gorgeous Elbow Cay, located only 26.1 km from Abaco Island. Both of these places are held in the greatest esteem by many families in Gulf County. They are treasured places that harbor beloved family memories. On September 1, 2019, Dorian slammed the cay of the Grand Bahamas at 04:40 p.m. It rated as the strongest known hurricane to impact the Bahamas. For about twenty-four hours, Dorian continued to wreak havoc. It would not move. While local residents watched the horror, they felt grateful that Michael quickly hit and left. Dorian refused to move as it sat over the same area for hours.

One year after Michael hit Gulf and Bay Counties, rebuilding continued while an island in the Atlantic was shredded. The brutality of this

TABLE 36

attack was like no other. Residents, who only a year earlier, bowed their heads with grief now watched, as, in another country, innocent people were brought to their knees. All around the two small towns of Mexico Beach and Port St. Joe, the words echoed. "How can we help? What can we do? So many helped us; we must not turn our backs on the Bahamas." Everyone felt helpless while they watched the brutal slaughter.

Such wonderful memories of long walks on sunny white beaches or spectacular sunrises and sunsets can never be forgotten in either place. Life continued as problems and grief pushed everyone forward. While survivors from Michael raised their eyes to the skies or shuddered to hear of another formation in the Atlantic, so do the Bahamians. We are joined with a common thread, pain and loss.

The suffering from neighbors in Abaco and all over the Bahamas stand as a reminder that no place is perfect. Disasters wait. Already, local planes are chartered and containers loaded not only with supplies for the people but for their pets. It is true, here in Gulf County, for a long time, tears continued to fall at memories. Thoughts of sweet meetings inside Sunset Coastal Grill or the weekly bridge games where laughter echoed from the walls just cannot be forgotten. Just as those in the Bahamas, now, mourn their losses and struggles and cope with insurance claims and never-ending cleanup, we of Gulf and Bay Counties understand what they are going through as do countless other hurricane survivors. Another disaster on some future date will replace Dorian that's true. Table 36 will be dwarfed by a new place where laughter will echo again, but we pledged never to forget life as it was while we pray God will help us never to lose compassion for our fellow man as we are forced to move forward.

All the brave men and women who suffered in the heat and humidity in the long summer days and nights of Florida and the Bahamas, to help a group of strangers, you represent all that we aspire to be, thank you. You are the best of mankind. To those who face indescribable losses in other brutal storms and disasters, we understand. You are not alone. We remember those who bravely stood with us. Now, we stand beside you.

AUTHOR BIO

Linda Heavner Gerald has received much acclaim for her books. She has been writing for over six years and published seventeen novels. Her work includes all genres. Linda writes each day with the goal of publishing books of substance. She draws from her medical background to alert her readers of current medical problems as well as providing inspiration through her many travels. Linda hopes to transport her readers from the safety of their home to places which they may never discover. Her most important goal is demonstrating that God loves all of us. Even though her characters create problems for themselves, she wittingly shows how God can extract us from the mess we make. The President's Book Award has been awarded several of her books for the past three years. This author has also obtained international acclaim. Linda's books are all over the world. Reader's Favorite bestowed the silver medal for her YA book, *AnnaPolis Summers* in 2018. In 2019, Linda won the Reader's Favorite Gold medal in Urban Fiction for the book: *Cycles Of Hatred*.

The Gulf of Mexico delights her as she shares her world with her husband, Buddy, of twenty-six years and their yellow cat, Jackson Brownie Gerald. Her son recently joined them in Florida, where the most beautiful beaches in the world welcome them.

Other Works By This Author

Betrayed In Beaufort
Rosemary's Beach House
Cycles Of Hatred
Dusty The Island Dog
Till Heaven Then Forever
Sins Of Summer
Confessions Of An Assassin
Murdered Twice
Enchanted
I Am Red
Claire's House
The Soldier And The Author
AnnaPolis Summers
VieVie La Fontaine
Dear John

Next Book

PERFECT

Linda Heavner Gerald

1

Miriam Kriegsman loved Benjy Tafeen from the moment she saw him when he transferred to her private Tallahassee school in the ninth grade. Her brown eyes sparkled with delight as she gazed on the handsome young man. Benjy's dark curly hair was surpassed in intensity only by his chocolate eyes. The smile he gave her took her young breath away. Never, had Miriam experienced such a deep stirring. As she looked into those eyes, which could melt stone, she curled her long thin dark hair around her thumb as she did when she felt nervous. His gay laughter told her that he understood the effect he had on her. Even at such a young age, Benjy knew he was a heart-breaker.

"Miss Kriegsman, *you* turn around and stop bothering Mr. Tafeen. Mr. Tafeen, *you* need to spend more attention listening to me then smiling at all of the young ladies around you." All the young ladies around Mr. Tafeen giggled as he leveled another of his devastating grins at his new fans. Benjy experienced the same reaction from the girls even in kindergarten. As their ninth-grade teacher, Mrs. Cone, smiled, the students immediately straightened-up. With a small grin, she explained the current lesson in Geography which included measuring distance on a map. "Who uses maps anymore? This is archaic." The kids all grumbled.

"You may say that David when you know how to measure and understand a map. They are still relevant!" Mrs. Cone sighed loudly. The kids spread the maps on their desks, while Miriam stole another stare at her "new boyfriend." At lunch that day, she didn't waste any time staking her claim to the most handsome guy in class.

"I don't know, Miriam. Benjy's a hunk. Although you're pretty, very pretty, he's so much more than handsome. He's dreamy. I would do anything to be his girlfriend."

Miriam glared at her best friend, Abbey. "Not me, I shall remain chaste for my future husband. No other man's hands may ever touch my pristine body." Abbey laughed at such a bold proclamation.

"Miriam, you're always so dramatic. I'll bet you aren't a virgin by the time you graduate high school. You better believe that Benjy won't be saving himself for *you.*"

The other girls laughed cheerily. It was for sure, Miriam was, indeed, a "drama queen." Since the young girl had never formally met this new student, her future love, she strolled over to the table of boys who pressed their heads together at lunch that day. Most likely, they discussed how to measure a map which they learned earlier in the day or maybe it was talk about the prettiest girl in class. Her friends gasped as Miriam marched toward the table of boys. It was true, most girls would never approach a table of boys but Miriam wasn't any girl. She thought of herself as a Jewish princess.

"Hi Benjy Tafeen. My name is Miriam Kriegsman and I'm gonna marry you someday." The young lad turned a bright red from his hairline to his chin as his buddies howled in joyous laughter. Miriam Kriegsman was a lovely girl but not exactly the sort the other boys loved to study and talk about; she was more of a geeky kid. Her thick glasses and small voice didn't attract the opposite sex like the beautiful Lila; a catchy Hebrew name which meant "night." The natural blonde was a bit of a phenomena among the school. Not only the color of her locks but the fullness of them often tumbled over her deepest green eyes. She was captivating. Miriam's thin mousey hair

TABLE 36

didn't compare but the two girls weren't on the same script. Lila kept many of the young boys awake at night as they dreamed ways to join her small group. None of them were ever invited.

Benjy avoided the spindly classmate for several weeks after her announcement. One thing about Miriam, she didn't sway easily. "Here, Benjy, I brought you chocolate rugelach. Mom made them yesterday. Do you like them?" After careful consideration, of how to steal his heart and several lame attempts, maybe she had hit the gold? Even Miriam began to feel a little defeated.

Chocolate rugelach happened to be his favorite dessert. Miriam's best friend, Abbey, had worked hard to steal this fact. Benjy's eyes stared at it in the same manner which his eyes lingered too long on Lila. Miriam had noticed the chemistry which existed between those two. Her commitment, to win his heart, remained undeterred.

"Gee, I don't know since I haven't tasted it yet." Benjy looked into Miriam's eyes. Then he turned to notice Lila observing his reaction. Still, that chocolate rugelach looked perfect.

"I'll just take a quick taste." He smiled at Lila who turned away in a pout. "Wow! Miriam, that's the best I've ever eaten. My Mom also makes it but hers aren't so chocolatey. Benjy quickly devoured the offering from the young girl. Miriam smiled at Lila with a gloat of the victor. A precedent of competitiveness between the two girls was set at that moment.

"Why don't you share lunch with me today? I'll give you two more of those. Would you like to join me? Just you and I will eat together. I'll lose my girlfriends.

Benjy hesitated but remembered that two of his favorite pals, Dan and Judd, were absent today. Both of them were scholastic giants and busy at a state science competition. He wasn't particularly fond of the remaining lunch partner, Mel.

"Well, I guess I can join you this one time but tomorrow, my best pals are back. You certain you have two full slices of the dessert for me?" He looked around the room a little nervously.

"Benjy, I have even more of a surprise. I hate the lunches here in the cafeteria so our maid, Hannah, makes my meals each day. Don't get lunch today, let me treat you to the best feast of your life!"

All through the morning, Benjy waited with high anticipation for the promised banquet. Even though Benjy and Lila hadn't spent a great deal of time together, there was an unspoken spark which united them. When lunch finally arrived, he gladly took Miriam's small damp hand as she led him to the table she claimed for their own. Lila watched in shock across the cafeteria.

Mel was outraged. "Hey Benj, you lost your mind? What you doin with Miriam? I thought you loved Lila. Besides, we always eat together!"

Hearing her name yelled into the air, the comely blonde child shook her head in horror as the only boy she cared for strolled with Miriam Kriegsman to begin a history of sharing lunches. Miriam lifted a designer backpack from the floor. It filled with delightful aromas. Everyone in the cafeteria watched as she carefully removed two large sandwiches of tasty spicy brisket served on a club roll. Sparingly, she poured a small amount of gravy over the concoction as the young chap wiped his mouth. There was only one thing Benjy liked more than a winsome lass. That was food.

Miriam couldn't take her eyes off him as he devoured the rather large club sandwich. His full pink lips curled up on the edges as he savored her gift. When a little gravy ran down his gin, she leaned forward and wiped it. "Oh, thank you, Miriam." Hesitantly, she pushed her lunch before him. Even though she dreamed of eating today, this was her favorite meal, she willingly gave it to Benjy.

"You sure? I mean, aren't you hungry?"

Miriam almost cried as she watched him unwrap her food, "I am but I want you to have this. I would give up anything to make *you* happy, Benjy. You can't imagine how much I think about you. Have you ever been so attracted to someone that you think about them all of the time?" The young girl couldn't remove her eyes from the chiseled, perfect face.

TABLE 36

Without missing a beat, as he hungrily unwrapped the second sandwich, he mumbled. "That's the way I feel about Lila. I'm crazy about her. You know?"

Although his words caused a little pain in the flat chest of his lunch partner; this youngster reasoned that, at least, he was truthful.

A pattern developed at that moment between the two. Miriam would suffer anything from Benjy. Any slip of his attention from her to another was always the fault of the other girl. Never, in her heart, did she hold him accountable for his flaws. Such behavior would be her undoing later.

2

By the time that the school finally closed the heavy scarred old doors for another summer, Benjy and Lila had become inseparable in their relationship. With great pride, Benjy had walked "his girl" to each class that year. Always, they stood together outside or enjoyed lively chatter by drivers to neighboring homes. All of these conditions appeared to line-up for their union someday. The only exception was Miriam. There was something about that girl Benjy couldn't explain to his friends. The young boy refused to reject her or exclude her from his world even though Lila and many others encouraged him to "move on."

For one year, Miriam provided lunch as she entertained "her boyfriend" with witty episodes from her prosperous family history. The young boy admitted to his friends that Lila was perfect in most everyway but not very challenging in one way for him. Her mental aptitude didn't cut it, whereas Miriam held similar intellectual concepts to his. The fit was perfect for Benjy and Miriam in that one regard. Poor Lila came up way short in the intellect department, but she seemed exceptional at math. She couldn't discuss current events, nor did she appear capable of deducting basic assumptions needed in daily life. Lila was beautiful and talented but seemed to be unable to communicate proficiently.

TABLE 36

As the students clambered to escape the stifling presence of teachers and long hours, they loudly discussed summer plans on this last day of the school year. "I can't believe summer is actually here. Miriam, what ya doing this summer?" Benjy walked with her because Lila wanted to say goodbye to a favorite teacher.

"Can you believe that my parents have signed me up for seven weeks at Camp Shalom? I go there each summer but usually only for two weeks. Don't get me wrong, I love it but seven weeks? Don't you think that's *too* much?"

"Oh, Benjy, let's go. Don't forget we're supposed to meet Mom at the club for tennis." The Venus strutted toward him with a broad smile. "What you guys talking about?" She glared at the other.

"Poor Miriam was telling me that her parents signed her up for seven weeks at Camp Shalom. What a shame."

Lila smiled, wickedly at the small girl. "Yes, it's *such* a shame. Miriam, Benjy and I talked about asking you to hang with us this summer, but I guess you'll be hanging at camp. Bummer! We sure will miss you." Through undisguisable laughter, the words echoed.

As the couple strolled away, Miriam wiped a tear from her eye as the tall blonde creature turned around to gloat. The night before, Miriam's mother forced her to pack early for summer camp, which didn't begin for another two weeks. During *that* time, Mrs. Kriegsman made arrangements for her only daughter to spend time in New York with grandparents. Not only was Miriam the light of our parents, but she was also their only child.

Often, the Kriegsman's discussed their child's obsession with this new boy named Benjy, to whom she constantly referred. Although money wasn't an issue, the amount they spent feeding him lunch each school day appeared bottom less. They weren't fond that Miriam appeared obsessed with him.

Most importantly, they had seen Lila and Benjy at dinners and other events. Seldom did the handsome boy even look at their daughter when walking beside the gorgeous blonde. It appeared he mostly enjoyed Miriam's company inside the school cafeteria where she fed him Hannah's treats. What waited for their child wouldn't be happy. They felt certain that heartbreak hid in the dark wings and hoped, by keeping her away from Benjy this summer, her attraction for the handsome lad may wane.

That very afternoon, with no time to herself, Miriam was whisked with her mother to the palatial home of New York grandparents. There, she cried herself to sleep each night while picturing Benjy and Lila kissing or sharing deep secrets. Her heart broke to see him again and hear his voice. Instead, her lunches were now planned with Josh Aaronson, whom she liked, but he wasn't Benjy. Day after day, Josh came to her grandparent's home as they swam together in the lavish pool and shared lazy lunches. He even taught her how to play an adequate game of tennis which made her think of Benjy and Lila laughing as they lobbed a ball over opponents. *Does he even think of me?* Miriam worried.

Back in Florida, Benjy *did* think of his friend, Miriam. In fact, he missed her spirit and the fun she added to his life. Both of his parents felt shocked when he began speaking of this particular friend and how much he missed her.

"Is he crazy? Have you seen the Kriegsman girl? Don't get me wrong, she is smart, funny, and successful just as Benjy describes, but she isn't Lila. Now that Lila is a looker!"

Personally, Benjy's Mom, Aliza, reveled in the fact that her son possessed such acute intellect. *Can he be so smart to realize that beauty fades but acumen is powerful? I hope, someday, he chooses Miriam. That girl will make a wonderful, loyal wife.* Never would she share these thoughts with her husband, Ron, who would have laughed.

"That boy won't settle down until way past college. He's got the lustful eye. I recognize it." Hilarity from the eyes of her husband met hers at the idea of such a silly thought that their handsome son may chose brains over beauty. *Is he remembering his own conquests?* There were plenty of those hanging in their closet.

TABLE 36

Sadly, Aliza looked at the giant rock of a diamond which covered her right ring finger. She had many such "trophies." Every time, Ron ended a relationship with a mistress or encountered a fling with one of his many women, her husband lovingly bestowed such a gift to her. There had also been lavish trips on yachts and other "trinkets" of his deep affection for his wife. Aliza always remained aware of what these invaluable treasures represented. Yes, heartbreak and disappointment waited for the wife of her handsome son. Part of her wanted to protect sweet Miriam. It would be better if Lila were forced to deal with Benjy's infidelities. That one seemed to possess a toughness. Aliza sighed as she considered the two young women caught up in a battle over her son.

Many miles away, Deborah Kriegsman's daughter dreaded her entry into summer camp. Arrangements had hastily been made by her parents to keep Miriam away for the entire summer. Benjy Tafeen had rung their doorbell the night before Miriam's departure. He begged to see Miss Kiegsman.

"Oh, I'm so sorry. Miss Miriam will be gone all summer, but we'll tell her about your interest." The maid closed the door in Benjy's face. The handsome lad walked away, missing his friend and wishing he could hear her small voice. The maid instantly alerted the Kriegsman couple to the unwanted visitor.

Made in the USA
Lexington, KY
31 October 2019